Mary Kate stalked after him, mentally berating him for his lack of cooperation, his arrogance, his conceit. There was only one way to gain his attention now.

"Mr. Taylor, how do you think the charges against you will affect your future?"

The question directed upward to the rock-hard jaw had scarcely left her lips when he wheeled around with a cold fury that rocked her back on her heels.

"I've lost a wife, my business is in jeopardy, and my self-esteem has been torn to shreds. I'm not sure I have a future." The blue eyes darkened in wounded pride, the rich voice faltering. "Now you've got your statement," he said wearily, as though the very life had been drained from him. "Are you satisfied?"

Mary Kate stood speechless, stepping back from the cutting blue gaze as he turned and walked away, the broad shoulders drooping.

"Hey, you were great," Coty lowered the camera, looking from her to the departing figure of Blake Taylor. "You captured his vulnerable side, and nobody's put that on film."

"Maybe," Mary Kate said, lifting a hand to massage the tense muscles in the back of her neck, "but I don't feel very proud of myself, Coty. In fact, what I feel is pure shame. I've never behaved so badly."

"Ah, come on! It takes guts to be a good reporter." Coty gave her a reassuring tap on the shoulder.

"Then maybe I just lost some of my ambition." Mary Kate hugged her arms against her chest, suddenly feeling a chill despite the warm day.

PEGGY DARTY is the popular, award-winning author of novels and magazine articles. Darty, who makes her home in Alabama, uses her extensive background in television and film to spin a tale of romance and intrigue that is sure to please all of her many fans.

Other books by Peggy Darty

HEARTSONG PRESENTS
HP143—Morning Mountain
HP220—Song of the Dove

Don't miss out on any of our super romances. Write to us at the following address for information on our newest releases and club information.

Heartsong Presents Readers' Service
PO Box 719
Uhrichsville, OH 44683

Summer Place

Peggy Darty

Heartsong Presents

A note from the author:
*I love to hear from my readers! You may correspond with me
by writing:* **Peggy Darty**
Author Relations
PO Box 719
Uhrichsville, OH 44683

ISBN 1-57748-319-7

SUMMER PLACE

All of the characters and events in this book are fictitious.
Any resemblance to actual persons, living or dead, or to
actual events is purely coincidental.

Cover illustration by Ron Hall.

PRINTED IN THE U.S.A.

one

"We have a story just breaking at the courthouse!"

Brad Wilson's announcement captured the attention of the staff at WJAK television newsroom.

"Is it the Blake Taylor story?" someone yelled.

Suddenly everyone was speculating again over the controversial trial. Was Blake Taylor, one of the most prominent developers in Florida, really a diamond thief? And when he had the money to buy the evidence that had been found in his home, why would he steal it? Or had he been framed by one of the competitors who had been irate over losing a million-dollar development to him, as the defense claimed?

The trial had stretched for weeks, while the city of Seabreeze buzzed with gossip. From the third desk back, Mary Kate Moore jumped to her feet, unable to endure the suspense.

"Well, tell us!" she cried.

All eyes shot to the petite woman who was flicking a strand of dark hair over her shoulder. The navy sailor dress fell loose about her slim ankles, further minimizing her slender, five-three frame.

Ignoring the stares of the more contained reporters, Mary Kate's gold-flecked brown eyes widened on the news director's face, imploring him to answer.

"Not guilty!" He finally reported, after holding his audience captive for a few tense seconds.

His reply was met by a moment of stunned silence. Then suddenly everyone was talking at once. How had Blake Taylor gotten off when the evidence had been found in his home? Was it the slick attorney, or had he really been framed?

Brad Wilson bounded across the room to Mary Kate's desk.

"Take Crew Three and get over there," he raked a nervous hand through his thinning brown hair. "There's another crew inside the courthouse getting interviews. Just try to get the reaction of the man on the street. And hurry."

"Right!" Mary Kate scrambled around her desk, grabbing a pen and pad. "Thanks, Brad," she added quickly, ignoring the envious gazes of other reporters as she stuffed the pen and pad into her large, navy shoulder bag and made a dash for the back door.

"She doesn't know how to walk," someone commented. "She always goes in a run."

"Maybe that's why she gets the stories," Brad replied with a caustic grin.

The words echoed in Mary Kate's ears as she reached the corridor, tossing a doubtful glance toward the closed doors of the elevator, then opting for the stairway instead.

"I get the stories because I work harder," she mumbled, flying down three flights of stairs and pushing the back door open. She blinked into the sudden glare of Florida's noonday sun as she headed across the parking lot. Seabreeze was located only ten miles from the ocean, and the balmy breezes drifted to the town, allowing a measure of relief on this hot day in August.

In the distance, the motor was already warming on the WJAK van, while Coty Brakefield stood loading the camera and Tom Allen worried over the sound equipment.

An amused grin tilted the corners of Mary Kate's pert mouth as she regarded the two men, so different in size and temperament, yet perfectly paired to orchestrate camera and sound into successful news coverage.

"Ready?" Coty's deep voice rumbled over the parked cars, his hazel eyes widening in his bearded face.

"Not guilty, can you believe it?" Mary Kate called in answer as she hurried across to the van, her gaze flicking over the big man dressed in khaki slacks and a loose T-shirt.

"Seabreeze is really buzzing," Tom informed them, folding trailing wires into the backseat. The smaller man, dressed more conservatively in dark pants and a plaid sports shirt, was checking out his equipment one last time.

"Come on guys. Hurry." Mary Kate climbed into the van. "But of course I don't have to tell *you* to hurry," she grinned at Coty. The gold flecks danced in her brown eyes as she glanced back at Tom jumping into the backseat.

"And no one has to tell *you* how to talk," Coty shot back, starting up the van and whipping the wheel around to make a U-turn. In seconds, they were roaring out of the parking lot.

"As long as she looks good on the tube, no one cares," Tom hung over the seat. "But you'd better brush your hair," he prompted under his breath.

"Give me time, Tom," she glanced over her shoulder, smiling. "I've had less than five minutes to grab my bag and make a mad dash to the parking lot."

As the men chuckled, Mary Kate flipped the visor mirror

down, examining her reflection critically. Her gaze lingered indifferently on wide-set brown eyes, sharply arched brows, rosy lips, and a complexion that remained smooth and flawless despite little care. Dark brown hair dipped in long waves about her oval face, and, as usual, it was in total disarray, thanks to her hectic schedule.

"Now where's my hairbrush?" she mumbled, diving into her shoulder bag. The jumble of contents within brought an impatient sigh, and she quickly tossed the bag on its side, dragging out each item in search of the elusive brush. A strange mixture composed of pens, pads, yellow stick-ons, a makeup bag, and a granola bar fell out. Another thump sent her New Testament, nestling in the bottom of the bag, to the floorboard.

"Uh-oh," Coty glanced back at Tom. "She's gonna try to convert us!"

Mary Kate looked up, puzzled; then catching Coty's eyes on her Bible, she grinned back. "Not right now, but I'd better get busy. The way *you* drive, I may not get many more chances."

Laughter rumbled from Coty's broad chest, and he accelerated even more, delighted by her squeal of fear.

She glanced at the buildings zipping past as they reached the heart of Seabreeze, a town of about sixty thousand. Glancing back into the visor, she gave up on the hairbrush and yanked a comb from her makeup kit. She dragged it through her thick dark hair in a few hasty attempts then shook her hair back from her face. It tumbled into deep waves that framed her delicate features and enhanced her classic bone structure. She managed to look both delicate and vulnerable, although she could be one of the toughest television reporters in the business. Her striking natural beauty captivated her television audience, but Mary Kate thought little about her beauty. She was far more interested in developing her inner self and devoted hours of reading self-help books in both her profession and her personal life. The small community church was an important part of her life, as well, and she attended regularly to strengthen her faith for the hectic days of her life.

While Coty often teased her about her religious beliefs, Mary Kate wondered how he and Tom, like so many others, could face life without the power available to them. She stared down at the cover of her New Testament before gently replacing it in her bag. Even a capsule prayer, at times like this, could provide her with a flash of wisdom and strength for the task ahead.

"Let's see what's going out over the wires," Coty's voice brought her back to the moment as he tuned in a popular radio station.

"It's ten o'clock in Seabreeze," a voice informed them. "The temperature is a sunny eighty-five degrees, with a slight breeze."

A wistful sigh escaped Mary Kate as she thought about spending a day at the beach, picnicking or sunning, or just loafing, doing some shopping.

"Listen," Coty nudged her, turning up the volume.

"This late bulletin just in," the casual voice tensed. "A verdict of Not Guilty has been handed down in the trial of Blake Taylor. Details later. . ."

"That's the first case the district attorney has lost in a long time," Coty wheeled around the corner, screeching to a halt near the crowd-jammed courthouse. "Ready?" he glanced at Mary Kate.

"Ready," she acknowledged, shoving the heavy door

open, then scrambling down, wondering why her instincts hadn't alerted her to wear slacks today.

"Where do you want to start?" Coty asked, the television camera hoisted to his shoulder. Tom, trailing behind, hugged cords and mikes.

Coty scanned the crowd, searching for those who looked willing to express an opinion.

"Look," Tom's voice halted them. "There's Blake Taylor coming out a side door."

Mary Kate's startled gaze flew to the distant figure. A well-tailored navy suit neatly encased broad shoulders and long legs, now stretched forward in a hurried stride. The man was making his way down the back steps in an effort to escape the waiting crowd in front of the building. His dark head was lowered in brooding contemplation.

Mary Kate recalled Taylor's other television appearances where he had entranced audiences with his rugged good looks, while the ice-blue gaze silenced noisy questions. He could be a real charmer, or he could slice a reporter to shreds.

Blake Taylor always looked cool and poised, despite the charges leveled against him. Shock waves had reverberated throughout the state when the prominent developer had been charged with the theft of a three-carat diamond ring, then a pair of ruby earrings and a matching ruby necklace. Soon, other items were found in his home, and nobody really expected him to beat the rap. He claimed to have an alibi during the robberies, and his alibi was substantiated by at least a dozen men who worked on a shopping center he was overseeing. But how did the jewels get into his house?

It was common knowledge that his wife, now deceased, had been dying of cancer. Public sympathy had almost been in his favor when one reporter suggested these were gifts for his dying wife, that her staggering hospital bills had all but bankrupted him.

The charges against him must have been a real blow to his ego. To approach him now, after the grueling trial, would be like stepping into the cage with a grizzly bear. And yet. . .

"Let's get a statement," she called over her shoulder, taking off across the courthouse lawn.

"Mr. Taylor," she called to him, not caring if Coty and Tom were keeping up as she ran as fast as she could.

He walked faster, ignoring her call, making no acknowledgment of her presence.

"Mr. Taylor!" Mary Kate yelled again, running to catch up, gulping for breath.

He whirled then, a threatening frown clouding his handsome face when he spotted the television camera on Coty's shoulder.

"Mr. Taylor, I'm Mary Kate Moore from Channel 6 News," she smiled brightly, although she was slightly out of breath.

He gave a brisk nod. "I made a statement earlier. I have nothing more to say." The rich voice was loaded with scarcely suppressed anger, matching the slash of dark brows and the steel glint in his deep blue eyes. Mary Kate swallowed, scrutinizing the broad-set jaw and jutting chin, marveling that a full mouth could be drawn in such a tight line. Only the look of soft brown hair offset the harsh planes of his face.

She felt a slight nudge between her shoulders and glanced back at Coty, closing in with the camera.

"Mr. Taylor," she blinked at him, inching closer, "can't

you just give us a few words? Aren't you pleased over the verdict?"

"Yes, and now excuse me!" he snapped, turning away.

"Wait!"

The desperation in her voice spun him around again, the eyes, blue stones now, chipping away at her self-confidence as he glared down at her as though she were a yapping puppy, blocking his path.

"The public deserves to hear *your* side of the story," she pressed further. "You've maintained from the beginning that you were innocent. Can't you elaborate why?"

He stopped walking and looked her squarely in the eye. "Because I *am* innocent. That's just been proven in a court of law. You can read the remainder of the story in the evening newspaper."

Mary Kate's mouth dropped open, his rudeness striking a raw nerve. If he could make a comment to the newspaper, why not to the television audience? This time her temper and her stubborn nature took over.

She threw an irritated glance at Coty who motioned her back toward Taylor, focusing the camera squarely on the tall man as the film continued to roll.

Mary Kate stalked after him, mentally berating him for his lack of cooperation, his arrogance, his conceit. There was only one way to gain his attention now.

"Mr. Taylor, how do you think the charges against you will affect your future?"

The question directed upward to the rock-hard jaw had scarcely left her lips when he wheeled around with a cold fury that rocked her back on her heels.

"I've lost a wife, my business is in jeopardy, and my self-esteem has been torn to shreds. I'm not sure I have a future." The blue eyes darkened in wounded pride, the rich voice faltering. "Now you've got your statement," he said wearily, as though the very life had been drained from him. "Are you satisfied?"

Mary Kate stood speechless, stepping back from the cutting blue gaze as he turned and walked away, the broad shoulders drooping.

"Hey, you were great," Coty lowered the camera, looking from her to the departing figure of Blake Taylor. "You captured his vulnerable side, and nobody's put that on film."

"Maybe," Mary Kate said, lifting a hand to massage the tense muscles in the back of her neck, "but I don't feel very proud of myself, Coty. In fact, what I feel is pure shame. I've never behaved so badly."

"Ah, come on! It takes guts to be a good reporter." Coty gave her a reassuring tap on the shoulder.

"Then maybe I just lost some of my ambition." Mary Kate hugged her arms against her chest, suddenly feeling a chill despite the warm day.

"Coty, we still have film left, haven't we?" Tom interrupted tactfully.

"Yeah, enough for another interview."

Mary Kate shook her head. "No, I'm finished. Let's go."

"What?" Coty stared at her.

"I said I'm finished," she replied miserably. "If you want to stalk the crowd for an opinion, go right ahead."

With that statement, she turned and trudged back to the van, guiltily recalling the manner in which she had pursued Blake Taylor, circling him mentally, analyzing his weakness, then swooping in like a vulture. She had sensed a vulnerable spot and gone for it, thoughtlessly and shamelessly. It was unlike her to be so callous and insensitive, but then he was the first person who had ever prodded her into losing her temper during an interview.

What was there about the man that set her so on edge? That made her violate the basic Christian principle of compassion? Talking tough was not Mary Kate's style, was not even consistent with her personal convictions. She operated from a code of ethics based on The Golden Rule.

She shook her head, forcing the corners of her mouth into a tense smile as she passed the crowd, but then the smile faded.

She owed Blake Taylor an apology.

two

"I think you're horrible!" the voice of an angry little girl shouted into Mary Kate's office phone.

Mary Kate gripped the telephone, wide-eyed, trying to ignore the noise of the newsroom in order to concentrate on her caller.

"I beg your pardon?" she managed finally. "Who's speaking?"

"My name's Hanna and you're a mean ol' reporter!" she repeated, more loudly this time. "You made Dad look awful on television last night and now he's left."

"Your dad?" Mary Kate frowned.

"Blake Taylor is my dad, and you made him feel awful. He's gone to our summer place at Seaside, and I'm going to run away, too. *I hate you!*" The little voice cracked a second before the phone clicked in Mary Kate's ear.

She shook her dark head, her thoughts spinning, as she replaced the phone and sat in a daze, trying to piece together the indignant message, shouted above the roar of a familiar noise she couldn't pinpoint.

Hanna Taylor. Blake Taylor.

She propped an elbow on her desk, cupping her chin in her palm as she lifted her thoughtful gaze to the far window, watching a dark cloud float past.

Searching her mind for information on the Taylor family, she recalled how the death of Charlotte Taylor—Mrs. Blake Taylor—had taken precedence over the local news shortly after Mary Kate had moved to Seabreeze to begin her new job.

Drumming her fingers on the desk, she scanned her brain for the newspaper article on Mrs. Taylor. Slowly, the story came back to her. She had been a fashion model who had made a name for herself before marrying Blake Taylor. Then she had stayed home with their child and apparently everyone had been happy until she was diagnosed with breast cancer. Surgery and radiation had not prevented the cancer from spreading to her bones, and she had died a painful death after a lengthy illness.

Mary Kate sighed, recalling the little girl's tormented voice. She hadn't realized when she prodded Blake Taylor to make his vulnerable reply that she would be hurting his daughter, as well.

"Brad—" she raised her eyes to her lanky boss, hurrying past her desk.

He whirled, brows arched questioningly.

"Brad, tell me more about Blake Taylor. I just got a complaint from his daughter about my interview."

Brad shrugged, raking a hand through his hair. "Taylor is a talented developer who put his unique brand of work on the new shopping center just west of town. He managed to retain a historical look to the center, while updating it with modern conveniences. Aside from his intelligence, I know nothing more. Oh, he and his wife lived in Tallahassee before coming here."

He fidgeted, eager to be gone.

"I see," Mary Kate murmured, her eyes narrowing as his words penetrated.

"Thanks."

Was it possible that a jealous competitor had planted the

jewels in his house, as he had claimed? His wife had certainly been too ill to shop, and the woman who worked for them was a plain type of woman, not given to fancy jewelry. And he had produced witnesses for his whereabouts on the days the jewelry had disappeared.

The phone pulled at her like a magnet, her clear-polished nails tapping a rhythm again on her cluttered desk. She ignored the papers, the work waiting to be done. She could not dismiss from her mind the voice of the little girl. The misery in that voice seemed to match the misery in her father's eyes.

"All because of me," she said, staring dejectedly at her nails.

"Get tough, Mary Kate," Brad had advised her on more than one occasion. "You'll never make it in this business if you take every interview seriously. Leave your work on the doorstep when you go home."

But home for her was a small duplex with only her cocker spaniel, Bo, waiting when she dragged in, hungry and tired. Her parents and older brother still lived up in Dothan, and she visited them as often as possible. She was a family person, not wanting to escape her roots, for she found real pleasure and companionship in being with her family. And yet, she had jumped at the chance to move to Florida and work at WJAK after graduating from college.

She rolled Brad's words over in her mind: *you'll never make it in this business if you take every interview seriously.*

Well, she had overstepped her boundaries, and her conscience was hounding her. She had to try and make amends; otherwise, she was not going to sleep very well tonight.

The dimension of caring that she brought to her work was the very ingredient that had set her apart from other reporters.

She believed it was why the public responded so easily to her. She owed Blake Taylor an apology and she was not above delivering it.

Taking a deep breath, she reached for the telephone directory, her fingernail making a sweep down the column of T's. Locating Blake Taylor's home and office number, she dialed the office, phrasing a conversation in her mind.

An efficient secretary informed her that Mr. Taylor was out of town for the remainder of the week.

Thanking the secretary, she hung up, recalling Hanna's last words: *I'm going to run away, too.*

What did she mean by that? she wondered, brows knitted. In the child's state of mind, that surely meant running away from home! She glanced at the wall clock. It was almost three-thirty. Hanna should be home from school by now.

Quickly, she dialed the home telephone number, tension building within her as she waited for an answer. Finally, a woman's voice came on the wire, announcing the Taylor residence.

"May I speak with Hanna, please?" Mary Kate asked politely.

There was a slight hesitation. "She isn't here. Who's calling?"

Mary Kate took only a second to ponder using a fictitious name, then in her typical straightforward manner, she replied honestly to the question.

"This is Mary Kate Moore."

"Mary Kate Moore? From WJAK?" The woman's voice was cold and flat.

"That's right."

"What do you want *now?*"

"I had a call from Hanna earlier," she explained, overlooking the woman's sharp tone. "I merely wanted to apologize."

Silence filled the wire before the woman continued in a more civil tone. "She hasn't come home from school yet."

"Not yet?" Mary Kate glanced at the clock again. "Isn't she running a bit late?"

"Well, this *is* the first week of school, and—wait a minute, what concern is it of yours?" she asked pointedly, as though remembering the interview again.

Mary Kate scooted to the edge of the chair, ignoring the small voice in her brain that warned her not to get involved. "May I come over, please? I think I should relate the phone conversation I just had with Hanna. I'm afraid there may be a problem and—"

"If you're looking for another story," the woman cut her short, "don't bother."

"I assure you that I'm *not* looking for another story," Mary Kate replied emphatically. "You have my word that none of this will reach the media."

"All right," the woman conceded. "I *am* worried, quite frankly. And Mr. Taylor has gone to his beach house for a few days' rest."

"Please give me your address." Mary Kate grabbed a note pad and reached for a pen. "I'll come right over."

After jotting down the address, Mary Kate ripped off the note and stuck it in the pocket of her white cotton slacks. Saying a hurried good-bye, she hung up the phone and grabbed her shoulder bag, making a dash for the back door. She paused as Carey, the secretary, shot her a questioning look.

"Carey, I'll be out for a while," she called over her shoulder.

"Oh? Want to leave a number?"

"No," Mary Kate forced a smile. "I just have to take care of some business."

Carey nodded thoughtfully, misinterpreting her words. "Have fun, then." Carey gave her an impish little grin.

Mary Kate merely smiled. Carey probably thought she was meeting someone. She decided to let it go that way. If Carey believed she were up to something, maybe she would quit trying to fix her up with her younger brother. Carey was a happily married woman with three children and wanted Mary Kate to find a good man.

She flew out the door and down the steps to the parking lot, the big door banging behind her as she stepped out into the warm afternoon.

She glanced up at the skies and saw a scattering of dark clouds. She remembered the weatherman had predicted rain this afternoon. By the time Mary Kate reached her red economy car, she was again feeling that nagging little concern for Hanna Taylor. Did she take an umbrella or rain jacket when she left for school? *If* she left for school. Or had she merely pretended she was going to school, then taken off someplace else? Surely she was all right, or she wouldn't be calling.

Mary Kate slid into the leather car seat and fished a silver ring of keys from her bag. As she inserted the key in the ignition and started the engine, she found herself pondering the wisdom of a trip to the Taylor home.

Why am I doing this? She wondered suddenly, a blank expression filling her brown eyes.

three

Mary Kate drove through town and turned into the exclusive area where Blake Taylor's home was located. She had continued to ask herself why she felt compelled to deliver Hanna's message in person. But she knew the reason. She was partly responsible if the child had run away.

"I've never been so insensitive in my entire career as a reporter," she said, into the silence of her car, as she stopped for a traffic light. She reached into her pocket, retrieving the note to verify the street and house number as the light changed and her mental argument continued.

Other reporters pursued, tantalized, aggravated. Such tactics seemed to go with the territory. But she was Mary Kate Moore, a Christian who lived by The Golden Rule and who attributed her small degree of success to her determination to live by her Christian standards.

She glanced around her, aware that she had reached the Taylors' exclusive neighborhood. Neat green lawns stretched past flower gardens to impressive homes of all sizes and shapes. Some ranch style, some Spanish, some Tudor. Rows of protective shrubs bordered the properties to ensure privacy. When she reached the mailbox marked 1507, she turned her car up the sweeping driveway to the quiet, Spanish-style home. Despite the pleasant white exterior and red tiled roof, the desperate stillness of the place brought a shiver racing down her spine as she parked the car and sat staring for a moment at the isolated house and grounds.

There were no shouts of playful children in the neighborhood, no vibrations from stereos or televisions, not even the sound of bike tires on the smooth pavement behind her. The neighborhood was depressingly silent, and she found it hard to imagine a normal, active child flourishing here, particularly one who had lost her mother.

Sighing, she reached for her shoulder bag and hooked it over her shoulder as she hopped out of the car. She followed the stone walk that curved past a manicured lawn that bore no evidence of children at play, up the circular steps leading to the front door.

Squaring her shoulders, she lifted her hand to the brass knocker and let it fall. The heavy thud magnified in her ears, while a low grumble of thunder echoed from the skies.

Slowly the door opened, and she stood facing a gray-haired woman, fiftyish and plump, her round face lined with concern.

"Hello," Mary Kate smiled. "I'm—"

"I know who you are." The woman gave a brisk nod and slowly opened the door. It was obvious she was reluctant to admit Mary Kate.

"And you're. . .?" Mary Kate extended her hand, determined to be friendly.

"Sue Sampson, the housekeeper. I've been with the Taylors for five years." Her work-roughened hand gripped Mary Kate's momentarily before retreating to her apron pocket.

"What did Hanna say to you over the phone?" she asked, closing the door behind Mary Kate. "And why did she call you?"

Mary Kate paused, studying the woman whose eyes held an expression of worry. She was scarcely taller than Mary

Kate, yet she was many pounds heavier, presenting the image of a motherly confidante.

"Well, I may be jumping to conclusions," Mary Kate began, wondering if she had overreacted to Hanna's phone call. She shoved her hands into her pants pockets, suddenly feeling ill at ease here.

"Come in," Sue said, her tone softening, as she led the way down a corridor and entered the second door on the right.

Mary Kate followed her into a large room painted a soft cream color, decorated in wines and deep greens in draperies and furnishings. The room was filled with overstuffed chairs and sofas and nice oak tables topped with brass lamps.

"We can talk here in the den." Sue motioned Mary Kate to a chair.

Mary Kate's heels sank into plush, deep green carpet as she took a seat in a chair. Glancing toward the cloudy sky, Sue turned on one of the lamps bringing a soft mellow glow to the room. Mary Kate's eyes returned to the clouds outside the window, and she decided to get right to the point.

"Hanna called to scold me about the interview with her father. And then she said, 'my father has gone off and now I'm running away, too.' Or something like that," Mary Kate shrugged, wondering if she had recited the conversation exactly as she had first heard it.

"Running away?" Sue gasped, scooting to the edge of her chair. "She didn't tell me she was going anywhere. Henry—that's my husband, he takes care of the yard work—has checked the neighborhood and didn't find her." She made no attempt now to hide her concern.

"Maybe it's only a threat," Mary Kate spoke gently, hating to bear the news. Still, something was obviously wrong; that was apparent after talking with Sue. "By the way, how old is Hanna?"

"She's eight," Sue answered absently, staring into space as though lost in thought. "After all we've been through—" she mumbled then bit her lip and broke off her flow of words.

Mary Kate suspected she was referring to more than today's problem. She cleared her throat. "Did she go to school today?"

Sue looked back at her and began to nod her head. "She got on the school bus this morning, but when she didn't get off this afternoon, I assumed she had stopped at Molly's house. That's her friend down the street. I just got off the phone with Molly's mother but she isn't there. Then you drove up. I thought maybe you knew something."

Mary Kate shook her head. "I've told you all I know."

Sue jumped up and rushed to the desk phone. "I'll call her teacher to see if she was at school today." She grabbed a small leather book and flipped it open. Then she began to punch the numbers into the telephone's keypad.

Mary Kate crossed the room and lifted a picture from a table, studying the face of a very pretty little girl. Perfectly chiseled features were framed by long blond hair. A pert nose hinted at mischief, but the smile was that of an angel. The eyes, a deep rich blue, reminded Mary Kate of those of Blake Taylor.

She returned the gold-framed picture to the table, her eyes lingering thoughtfully on the little girl's face. While she had beautiful eyes, they did not reflect the confidence of her father. Perhaps that air of assurance would come in later years, after she had solved the mysteries of her own little world.

"She didn't go to school today!" Sue cried, dropping the

phone awkwardly before scrambling for it, then replacing it on the hook. "She may have run away, like you said." She sank into the desk chair, obviously stunned.

Mary Kate moistened her lips, searching for something comforting to say, and yet she knew that Sue had every right to be distraught. "Children often run away just to prove something. Then they're back home by dinner. Maybe that's what Hanna will do."

She heard the sound of fear in her own voice and realized even as she attempted to calm Sue, that other fears, worse fears, were forming in her own mind.

A vulnerable little girl running away from home was bad enough. When that little girl was the daughter of a prominent developer who could pay a hefty ransom. . .

"I've had a sick feeling in the pit of my stomach all week," Sue's voice trembled. "Mr. Taylor's been so involved with the trial that he's hardly had time to speak to the rest of us. Hanna has seemed so lonely lately." She jumped to her feet, reaching for the phone again. "Why am I sitting here rambling? I've got to call Mr. Taylor."

"He's at his beach house, you said?"

Sue nodded. "On the upper end of the beach where it's quiet. Hanna begged for him to wait until the weekend so she could go with him, but he was so worn out after the trial, he said he needed a few days to himself. Hanna didn't understand," she sighed, clutching the phone, waiting for an answer.

Mary Kate thought it over. Since Seabreeze was only a short drive from the beach, Blake Taylor could be back home in twenty minutes or so.

"I have an appointment soon," Mary Kate glanced at her watch. "I must go. If you or Mr. Taylor need to reach me, I'll be at the station until seven. After that, I'll be at my apartment." She removed a business card from her purse. "Here are both numbers, office and home phone."

Sue Sampson nodded bleakly. "You will respect our privacy?" she asked desperately.

"Of course I will," Mary Kate reached across the desk to touch her hand reassuringly.

"Mr. Taylor?" Sue spoke the name into the phone then glanced cautiously at Mary Kate.

Tactfully, Mary Kate turned and hurried out of the den. She could hear Sue's voice speaking in a low tone as she crossed the foyer and let herself out the front door.

If Blake Taylor had been notified, then there was nothing more she could do. Except pray. Once she stepped out into the gray afternoon, she looked up at the clouds. It was going to start raining any minute now. Where was Hanna? Her eyes scanned the neighborhood as she hooked her shoulder bag over her arm and crossed the porch.

There was something terribly depressing about the surroundings here, or perhaps it was only the gloomy day. Still, her steps quickened as she hurried back to the car. She was suddenly anxious to get away.

෴

Mary Kate sat on the edge of a chair in the darkened editing room going over last week's interview with a local politician. The interview had been one of her typical, on-the-street clips, but this one had been unique in that she had captured the man and his son on their way into a fast-food establishment.

They had spent a few seconds discussing the merits of hamburgers and french fries for growing boys before the politician adeptly maneuvered the conversation back to his upcoming election.

"He's a cool one," the film editor commented as he

checked the frames, "but he lacks something."

"Charisma, Bill," Mary Kate nodded. "I noticed that too."

"Too bad Blake Taylor doesn't run for office," Bill offered idly, unaware that the name had brought Mary Kate upright. "Now there's a man with plenty of charisma. Talked his way right out of that theft charge."

Mary Kate frowned. "Do you believe he was guilty?"

Bill shrugged. "That slick attorney's argument of a jealous competitor planting the jewels didn't convince me."

Mary Kate chewed her lip. "But he had airtight alibis during the time the jewelry was stolen."

Bill gave her a sardonic grin. "Mary Kate, that man can buy plenty of alibis!"

She stared at him, weighing his words. Was it possible? Her thoughts darted back to Hanna. She wondered if the little girl had been located. In front of her, the footage of the politician ran on, and she forced her eyes back to the screen. As she stared at the blond politician, she saw in his place the dark commanding presence of Blake Taylor.

Bill's right about his charisma, Mary Kate thought, recalling how she had stood mesmerized on the courthouse steps before she could propel herself into action.

She stood up, her nerves on edge. "I think that looks okay, don't you, Bill? If Brad agrees, we'll use it one night this week."

"Yeah, it's okay." Bill flicked the lights on, grinning across at her. "You're the one who should run for office, you know. You have a way with people."

Mary Kate waved a hand of dismissal at his teasing grin. Bill liked to goad her for fun, telling her that her successful interviews were aided by her good looks and charm. It usually prompted a healthy argument between them, but she ignored him now. She hadn't the time for more jostling. She prided herself on her ability to create rapport with the person on the street. It would have been a compromise of her convictions to use feminine wiles rather than intelligence and skill.

She hurried back down the corridor to the newsroom. Brad's deep voice halted her as she rounded a corner.

"Mary Kate! I took a look at the footage on that Jenkins guy. Good job!" He caught up with her, giving her a nod of approval as they walked back to the newsroom.

"Mr. Jenkins was a delightful interview," she smiled up at Brad. "Can you imagine yourself walking five miles a day when you're eighty-three? He never misses a morning, he told me."

Brad groaned. "I can't force myself to do two miles a day at forty-two!" His lanky stride slackened at the thought. "No discipline, that's my problem."

Mary Kate laughed. "Well, you easily cover a dozen miles a day just pacing around this building." They turned into the wide door of the newsroom.

"Mary Kate! You're wanted on the phone," Carey called. "Some kid."

Mary Kate's mind bolted to the memory of Hanna as she raced across to the desk, scrambling for the phone.

"Didn't know you were so fond of kids," Carey called with a grin.

She gave Carey a quick smile as she sat down at her desk and forced a calm tone to her voice as she lifted the receiver.

For a moment there was no reply to her hello, just light breathing.

"Hello," Mary Kate repeated. "Who's there?" She gripped the phone tighter.

"You didn't tell them I'd run away."

Mary Kate blinked for a moment, too confused by the words to grasp their meaning at first. "Is this Hanna?" she asked. Then she thought she knew what the little girl meant. "Who was I supposed to tell?"

The little girl huffed an impatient sigh. In that quiet second, a public address system announced a twenty-five percent discount on a special brand of electric trains.

Mary Kate gripped the phone tighter, listening, aware that her caller was in a large store. But which one? Her eyes flew to the glass window, and she saw that it was pouring rain and day was giving way to early evening.

"You didn't announce it on television!" Hanna stated slowly, emphatically, as though being sure she made her point.

Mary Kate concentrated on her words, her mind probing for the proper replies. "Did you want me to?" she asked softly.

There was a slight hesitation again, a vibrating hum filling up the silence as Mary Kate closed her eyes, struggling to remember where she had heard those sounds before.

"Well, I *have* run away!" Her voice rose in an indignant protest. "Not that anybody cares!"

"Hanna, listen to me," she took a deep breath, praying for the right words. "Everyone cares about you. Everyone is worried. You need to call home right now."

Another impatient sigh.

"Listen," Mary Kate continued, wondering if she had time to put a tracer on the call, "I'm really sorry about that interview. I upset your father and that's why he went away. It wasn't because of you, and now he'll be sick with worry. You don't want to do that to him, do you?"

"He doesn't care. All he cares about is his business."

Mary Kate gulped, searching for another argument. "Sue is

terribly upset. You need to call her right this minute. She's—"

"Sue doesn't care either. She's always talking to her daughter on the phone. She never has time for me."

Mary Kate gasped, feeling her heart go out to this poor lonely child. Somehow she had to think of the right words to reach her.

"If you'll just come back home, you'll see that you're wrong and—"

"No! I'm never going home," she threatened, her voice trembling.

Mary Kate's eyes flew back to the window, watching the rain pour down.

She was making a desperate mental plea to God for a way to help Hanna. Then during that moment of silence, she could hear the public address system and this time the message was distinct.

"Stop in at the Wun-der-ful World of Toys for all your children's needs."

She bolted upright in her chair. "Hanna, if I can get a special news bulletin about you on the air in the next half hour, could you watch it? Is there a television set nearby?"

"Yeah. I can see a television set where I am," she replied slowly.

"Great!" Mary Kate was already getting to her feet, reaching for her shoulder bag.

"You stay right where you are and watch that television. I'll try to get that bulletin on within the next half hour. Okay?"

"Okay! But make it good," she added, a note of triumph in her little voice.

"I will. Don't go away from that television set!"

As soon as the line clicked, she hung up to break the

connection. Then she quickly lifted the phone again, her fingers zipping over the numbers as she punched in the Taylor residence. A rich male voice answered on the first ring, and she realized with a start that Blake Taylor had returned.

"Mr. Taylor?" she asked tentatively.

"Yes? Who is this?" he barked impatiently.

"This is Mary Kate Moore. I think I've located Hanna." The words burst from her throat.

"What? How? The police are looking everywhere."

"She just telephoned me wanting to know why I hadn't broadcast her runaway over the news. I distinctly heard a public address system announcing sales at the Wun-der-ful World of Toys. I'm sure that's where she is."

This was a huge toy store in the mall, featuring items of interest for kids of all ages, with a special set of colorful televisions, guaranteed to match any color scheme.

"I thought the police checked the mall three blocks away. There's a Wun-der-ful Toy store there."

She rushed on. "When I asked Hanna if she could watch a television if I put on a special news bulletin, she was quick to assure me that she could. I think you'll find her in that special little television department. I'm going there now," she added, unwilling to waste more time. "Good-bye."

"I'll meet you," he yelled in her ear as she replaced the phone and hurried toward the door.

"Take an umbrella," Carey shoved a small black one toward her.

"Thanks, Carey. What would I do without you?" she called over her shoulder, as she darted out of the newsroom.

&

Mary Kate drove through the slashing rain, trying to be

careful as darkness began to descend over Seabreeze. In exactly fifteen minutes, she had reached the parking lot near the huge toy store at the mall. The rain had slackened a bit, but it was still a miserable afternoon.

Grabbing the dripping umbrella, she opened the door and hopped out. Sidestepping the mud puddles, she huddled under the umbrella, nodding her thanks to a car that waited for her to pass.

She rushed to the front door, lowered the umbrella, and entered the brightly lit department store, a stark contrast to the dark afternoon. She was familiar with the layout of the store, and she took a shortcut through Little Guys Tools and cut around the floor-to-ceiling shelves of dolls where she slowed down, peering around a life-size doll to the entertainment center. What she saw melted her heart.

Blake Taylor, in khaki shorts and sports shirt, was kneeling beside a stool where a blond head was nestled into his shoulder. His arms were wrapped around the little girl, and he, too, looked as though he were about to cry.

She hesitated. There was no point in intruding on a family matter. He had found his daughter, that was all that mattered. She was about to turn when Blake's moist blue eyes lifted over Hanna's head, widening suddenly at the sight of Mary Kate. She gave him a little smile then lifted her hand in a reassuring wave. Quickly, she turned and headed back toward the door. She knew Hanna would think she had betrayed her, and she was sorry for that. But she was glad she had been reunited with her father, and maybe everyone had learned a lesson.

"Could I help you?" asked a voice from behind her.

She jumped, whirling to face an equally surprised salesman.

"Hey, you're the girl who does the on-the-street interviews, aren't you?"

The older man's eyes widened with interest. "Are you looking for a special toy? Or someone to interview?"

She smiled. "No, I was just leaving," she replied politely and hurried through the door into the light drizzle. The night sky was slowly beginning to clear, and she decided that was a good omen.

four

Remembering her hasty exit, Mary Kate decided to check in at the office before going home for the night. Brad, who seemed to eat and sleep in his glass-enclosed office, was working late. As she passed his door, he gave her a silent salute, still cradling the telephone against his shoulder.

Waving back, Mary Kate hurried on, hoping she had misinterpreted the look of quiet panic on his face. Clearing her desk, then locking the drawers, she was preparing to leave when she caught a glimpse of Brad's long legs swiftly closing the distance between them.

"Aren't you overdoing your dedication to WJAK?" he asked teasingly. Before she could answer, he plunged on. "Hal's sick and the drugstore on South Main is on fire." He waved a scribbled note. "Crew Three is covering. Could you go, Mary Kate? We'll hold a slot on tonight's wrap-up."

"But—" Her brown eyes widened in protest as she stared up into his pleading face. Then her protest died in her throat as she glanced around the deserted newsroom.

"Okay, but you're a tough boss, Brad!" She yanked the piece of paper from his hand, whirling for her shoulder bag. "You know I don't like fires."

Her lips thinned in frustration as she checked her purse for her pen and pad, then took off. A nagging voice within reminded her that it had taken two years to earn the distinction of being one of the station's best reporters. If she wanted to protest overwork, she must do it later in a more businesslike manner. *A point of discussion tomorrow,* she vowed, glancing over her shoulder at Brad. He was back at his desk, slumped in the chair, the phone cradled against his ear.

She trudged out the door, her small chin thrust forward in defiance. *Tomorrow,* she vowed. *But for now there's a building on fire!*

♨

Exhaustion crept into every bone in Mary Kate's body as she dragged herself up the steps to her duplex. The hour was late and she longed for a leisurely soak in the tub followed by twelve hours of uninterrupted sleep. The phone was ringing as she unlocked the door. Hurriedly flipping on the light in the foyer, she dashed toward the nearest phone and tripped over a discarded house shoe from the morning's hurried departure. *I have got to slow down!*

"Hello," she shouted irritably, cradling the phone against her shoulder as she leaned over to drag her sandals from her aching feet. Frowning at the blister on her big toe, she was caught momentarily off guard by the rich masculine voice on the other end of the wire.

"Ms. Moore? This is Blake Taylor." He spoke slowly. "I hope I'm not bothering you."

She snapped upright, surprised by his call. "No, that's okay. How's Hanna?"

"She's fine," he answered politely. "I didn't get a chance to thank you earlier."

She blinked and sank into the sofa, reaching for the lamp on the end table. "I'm just glad I could help," she replied, turning the switch and focusing on the circle of light on her carpet. Her thoughts moved on to Hanna and again she felt guilty. "Would it be possible for me to speak to Hanna? I think I owe her an apology. I sort of. . .betrayed her, I suppose."

"She's already in bed," Blake hesitated, "and it might be better to wait. She is a bit upset with you, but then she's been upset with everyone. I hope you understand. She's just a child, after all."

"I do understand." Mary Kate closed her eyes, thinking of the vulnerable little voice that had begged for attention. "Where was she all day? Did you find out?"

"I think she just wandered around the mall, somehow managing to elude everyone who was looking for her. The minute Sue called, I rushed back home. We were frantic," he added, the tension returning to his voice.

"Well," Mary Kate sighed, "I'm glad she's home safely, Mr. Taylor."

"Blake," he added gently. "Since you've been involved in our family trauma, we should at least be on a first-name basis."

"About the interview," she continued, wanting to make amends so that she could ease her conscience. "I really don't know what came over me. I've never been such a pest during my career as a reporter. I'm sorry."

"You were merely doing your job," he answered after a momentary pause. "I respect that, even if you were doing that job on *me*." He was chuckling softly into the phone.

Mary Kate's brow lifted. So he had a sense of humor, after all. "Well, I think I overdid my job, as you put it. I had no right to provoke you that way."

"Let's just forget the entire incident. I was overwrought from the trial. We've been through a strain. I'm sure you can appreciate that. I'd like to put the matter behind me."

"I'll be happy to join you in that," she replied.

"Now back to my reason for calling. I wanted to invite you

to dinner at our house tomorrow evening. Would you join us—Hanna and me? The poor kid is pretty embarrassed about everything. I suppose that's normal."

"I suppose." Mary Kate bit her lip, wondering if anything Hanna had done could be considered normal.

Dinner? With Blake Taylor? And his troubled daughter? She frowned.

His deep voice filled her ears again, this time more persuasive. "I feel we owe you something. Please allow us to make amends. Even Sue insists on preparing a nice dinner for you."

Mary Kate took a deep breath, thinking there was no way she could refuse. "All right, but my work schedule won't allow me to be definite about the hour, I'm afraid. The best I can do is get there between six-thirty and seven. Is that okay?"

"That's fine. Just come when you're free. I'm taking the day off. I intend to spend more time with Hanna. I've learned something from all this, I hope."

His relief at having his daughter back was evident.

"Perhaps we all have," she replied. "Enjoy your day with Hanna, and I'll see you tomorrow evening. Good night. . . Blake." She replaced the phone and stretched out on the sofa.

Mary Kate lay still, savoring the peaceful moment and thinking about the Scripture verse which promises that all things work together for good to those who love God and are called according to His purpose. Perhaps the temporary anguish suffered during Hanna's disappearance had been worth the cost.

Her brown eyes drifted toward the ceiling, a smile lighting her weary features.

"Thank you," she whispered.

five

"A wrap!" Coty nodded, lowering the camera.

"Thanks, kids." Mary Kate smiled at the students at Winston Elementary who had agreed to be interviewed about an upcoming bake sale and car wash. They were working hard to help one of their teachers who needed a kidney transplant. It had been a touching story.

She unhooked the microphone and waved to the group. "You can see yourselves on the news at five o'clock tonight."

Her little audience whooped their response, then dashed off to join the line at the side entrance of the school.

"Whew, what a day!" She glanced at Coty as they climbed back into the van.

"Like every other one," he answered, wedging his considerable weight in under the wheel.

She leaned back in the seat, closing her eyes in an effort to relax as Coty started the van and they spun away from the curb. She had spent a hectic morning rushing from one location to another, Brad thrusting an assignment in her face each time she slowed down to catch her breath. While she had performed her tasks with the usual diligence, one part of her consciousness centered on Blake and Hanna, each presenting a different problem.

She prayed that Hanna had forgiven her and that this dinner together would somehow make things right between them. Reaching for her shoulder bag, Mary Kate remembered the two Sea World tickets she had been given as a member of the press. Maybe Hanna would want to go. Regaining her trust would not be easy, but perhaps she could make a beginning.

She thought of Blake Taylor again, wondering why the man lingered in her mind. She had lain awake last night, despite utter exhaustion, debating whether this nervousness was connected to her concern for Hanna or the strange effect he had on her. Blake Taylor set her nerves on edge, like a flash of lightning streaking through a summer sky.

Coty swung into the parking lot and was turning off the engine of the van as she roused up in her seat, a weary yawn escaping her.

"I've had a craving for Mexican food all day," Coty glanced at her. "Want to try that new place over on Union Street?" He reached into the backseat for his camera.

"Nope. I don't have that kind of craving."

"Well, what's next?" he nodded toward the clipboard in the front seat.

"This is it, I hope." She pressed a hand to her forehead, fighting off the dull ache there.

"Can you rush that film over to Editing so they can see how it looks? In the meantime, I'll check my desk for messages. Thanks, Coty, and I'll take a rain check on the Mexican food."

She gathered up clipboard and purse and climbed down from the van. Hurrying across the parking lot to the back door of the station, she prayed this would be her last assignment for the day.

Deep in thought, she stepped through the slow-moving doors of the elevator and absently punched the button, watching the lights flick on the floor numbers as the elevator swung upward. She looked over her still-fresh white silk blouse and navy slacks, deciding that it would not be necessary to change before going to the Taylor home for dinner.

Stepping off the elevator, she headed for Brad's office, ready now for that confrontation about her overloaded schedule. Nothing was going to prevent her from keeping her date this evening, she decided.

ða

Later, when Mary Kate arrived at the Taylor house, her neat appearance belied her hectic day. Her efforts to convince Brad that she was overworked had been waved aside with a rash of compliments and a cunning grin. Still, her work load *had* lightened, and now she was arriving before dark, like any other respectable dinner guest.

Hurrying up the walk to the front door, a cooling breeze wafted over the green lawn, bringing with it the pleasant aroma of meals being prepared in the neighborhood. She took a deep breath, settling her hand onto the top of her shoulder bag as she waited.

The front door swung open and Sue stood smiling, her hazel eyes reflecting a pleasant expression this evening.

"Come in, Ms. Moore!"

"Thank you. And please call me Mary Kate," she smiled, stepping into the foyer. She had changed out of her working sandals into dressy navy pumps, freshened her makeup, and brushed her hair. But suddenly she wished she were more. . . sophisticated. . .or glamorous.

You're Mary Kate Moore and that's good enough, she scolded herself.

"Mr. Taylor and Hanna are in the den," Sue indicated with a nod. Then her eyes swept over Mary Kate's white silk blouse and navy slacks and returned to her face. There was an inscrutable expression in her eyes, which left Mary Kate to wonder what she was thinking before Sue turned and led the way to the den.

"Thank you," Mary Kate absently brushed a speck of lint from the sleeve of her blouse. Sue paused in the doorway, announcing that their guest had arrived, and Mary Kate had a brief glimpse of father and daughter seated at a checkerboard in intense concentration before both heads spun in her direction.

"Come in," he stood, motioning her to join them.

Hanna's little cheeks colored slightly and she jumped up, ready to make a dash from the room. Blake's hand reached out, gently drawing her against him.

"Wait, Hanna," he said quietly. He was casually dressed in tan slacks and a pale blue polo shirt, emphasizing his brown hair and blue eyes. Hanna wore a pink shorts outfit.

"Hello Hanna," Mary Kate smiled, hoping to make friends despite Hanna's obvious unwillingness. She reached into her purse and withdrew the tickets. "I have two passes for Sea World—"

"I don't want to go," Hanna glared at her.

"You don't? Have you ever watched a baby dolphin play?"

Mary Kate's gaze slipped to Blake who stood observing the parley between them in quiet amusement.

"No. . ." Hanna's tone softened, curiosity and excitement overcoming her anger.

"Then you should definitely visit Sea World. It's lots of fun." Mary Kate smiled warmly, ignoring the child's impolite manner. "I'll bet you a giant bag of popcorn that you'd have a good time, Hanna."

"Sounds great to me," Blake beamed at Mary Kate, his approval obvious. "What about you, Hanna?"

Hanna merely shrugged and dropped her eyes to the floor in sullen silence. Just then Sue appeared in the door to announce dinner, and Mary Kate smothered a sigh of frustration.

"Yes, I think we're all ready for one of your delicious dinners, Sue." Blake's broad shoulders drooped slightly as he glanced from Hanna back to Mary Kate. "How about you?"

"Definitely," she nodded, trying to recall what she had eaten for lunch and deciding she must have forgotten to eat.

"Then what are we waiting for?" Blake smiled at her.

Mary Kate stared for a moment. It was the first time she had seen him smile, and she was more than a little dazed by the effect of white teeth against suntanned skin, offset by the clearest, deepest blue eyes she had ever seen. Except for his daughter's eyes. She glanced back at Hanna.

The little girl had tilted her face to peer sideways at Mary Kate. Once their eyes met, her glance darted away.

With his arm around Hanna's shoulder, Blake led the way into the dining room. Mary Kate followed, wondering how to bridge the awkward silence with the little girl. *This is not going to be easy.*

The formality of the dining room seemed to add to the starched atmosphere. Blake seated Mary Kate at the opposite end of the table, with Hanna to her right.

Mary Kate tried to force an appreciative smile at the sight of the snowy linen tablecloth, the gleaming silver, the elegant china. The corners of her mouth refused to budge, however. It occurred to her that a cozy kitchen supper would have been easier for her first meal with Blake and Hanna. They would all have been more relaxed. Or did these two ever relax? she wondered.

Leaning back against the ornate mahogany chair, she stole a glance at Hanna, slumped over her plate. She seemed smaller and more vulnerable than ever with her thick blond hair hanging about a too-thin face. Mary Kate realized the picture she had seen in the den was a recent one. Hanna had not changed, except for losing more weight.

She turned her attention to the platter of roast beef that Sue was placing on the table. "My, that looks good," she said, watching a parade of accompanying dishes—carrots, creamed potatoes, green beans.

"I hope you enjoy everything," Sue replied, glancing at Mary Kate with that same peculiar expression before she turned and hurried back to the kitchen.

Blake took a sip of water, his eyes meeting hers over the rim of the crystal goblet. Shaken by a jolting awareness of his masculinity, Mary Kate busied herself with the white linen napkin. It felt clean and crisp against her fingertips. She wondered if he were going to offer grace, then realized he was not when he began to speak.

"Well, tell us about yourself. How did you happen to get into television reporting?"

"Almost by accident," she replied, warming to one of her favorite subjects. "I started out as a part-time reporter for an Alabama television station. I worked during the summers while I attended college. Then after college, I went back full time. I was an anchor on the evening news when Brad—my boss here—was passing through town and caught the telecast. He came by the station the next day and offered me a job." She shrugged lightly, hoping she didn't sound too boastful. "It was merely luck."

"You're doing a good job," Blake said as Sue served the food. "We watched you on television covering that fire at the drugstore. Aren't you nervous about covering an assignment like that? I mean, it could get dangerous, couldn't it?"

She studied the silver meat fork as she lifted a slice of roast beef onto her plate, then added vegetables. "Fires definitely are not my favorite news story," she acknowledged with a grin. "But one of our top reporters is on vacation, leaving the rest of us to pick up the slack." She took a sip of water.

"I think you're being modest." Blake watched as Sue filled his coffee cup from a silver pot. "I've noticed you're covering some pretty important people and events."

"Actually, my specialty is on-the-street interviews. I like talking with the average person, trying to find something fresh and exciting in everyday life. I don't have any strong desire to get into hard news."

"That's very commendable," he nodded, sipping his coffee. "My experience with reporters has often been unpleasant, due to their efforts to make a flashy report rather than an accurate one."

While his remark had been innocently stated, the tense silence that followed hung thickly over the table, as the three of them recalled her brief interview with Blake only days ago.

She lowered her eyes, wondering if she had blundered terribly by even discussing her work.

"Why were you so mean to my dad?" Hanna blurted, glaring at her.

"Hanna—" her father started to scold her.

"No, that's okay," Mary Kate put up her hand. "That's a fair question, and I think we need to talk about that." She took a deep breath. "Hanna, I have apologized to your father, and now I would like to apologize to you. I was tired and rushed and—" she broke off, realizing she was not being honest. "That's just an excuse. I guess I wanted a story and your dad was outsmarting me. I lost my temper. Please forgive me."

"And you tricked me!" she lashed out, tears filling her blue eyes. "You told me I was going to be on television, but instead you called my dad." She jumped out of her seat, sloshing the water from the crystal goblet.

"Hanna," her father called sternly.

She paused at the door, her little shoulders set in a rigid line.

Mary Kate looked at Blake and shook her head. It had turned into a terrible scene, and she was more embarrassed for the Taylors than for herself.

Blake's eyes rested on Mary Kate. "Don't fuss at her," she mouthed quietly.

His eyes swept back to his daughter. "You're excused, Hanna," he said in a low voice.

She darted from the room.

"Actually," Mary Kate said quietly, "she has every right to be upset with me."

"But no right to be rude, when I specifically asked her to behave tonight." Blake dropped his eyes.

As Mary Kate looked down the table to him, she was startled to see this touch of vulnerability on a man who had achieved so much success. Apparently, life at home was a different story.

Mary Kate picked up her fork and began to push her food around her plate, but her appetite was gone. Soon even Blake made no pretense. The room was silent when Sue entered later, to check on them.

"Is something wrong?" she asked, looking from one to the other.

"The meal is wonderful, Sue." Blake sighed. "Hanna's behavior altered our appetite, that's all. Would you mind leaving the food in the oven? Maybe we'll have a snack later."

He looked down the table to Mary Kate. "How about coffee in the den?"

She nodded. "I'd like that."

She laid her napkin across the table and stood, smiling sadly at Sue. "Your food was wonderful," she said, glancing back at her scarcely touched portion. "I'm sorry," she added.

Sue began to nod her head. "I understand."

Mary Kate decided if Sue had worked here for a while she must be accustomed to the family's problems. She followed Blake back to the den and tried to clear her mind by looking over the book-lined room. The variety of books on the shelves reflected the personality of an intelligent, well-read man. She moved to the floral sofa and took a seat as Blake settled in the recliner opposite her. Sue entered with a tray holding a pot of coffee and two china cups.

"I'll pour. Thank you, Sue."

Blake walked over and poured the rich dark brew into the cups then glanced at Mary Kate. In the soft glow of the lamps, his eyes were an even deeper blue. "Sugar or cream?" he asked.

"Just black, thank you." She looked away, mentally telling herself that she must not become involved with this man and his daughter. And there was still the matter of the stolen jewelry. *What was the real story?* she wondered, as her heart beat faster.

She took the cup from his hand, feeling the warm brush of his fingers. Something told her to run for her life before she lost her heart. Then as she looked up to thank him, she felt her heart give a leap and she wondered if it was already too late.

"You're really good with children," he said, settling back on the sofa and studying her thoughtfully. "Do you come from a large family?"

She smiled, warmed by the thought of her rowdy brothers and sister. And yet they had always had such a good time together. "As a matter of fact, I do. I have three brothers and one sister. I'm next to the youngest."

"Where did you go to college?"

"The University of Alabama in Tuscaloosa. And you?"

"The University of Tennessee in Knoxville. I was a business major. Guess I always knew I wanted to be in real estate. That was my minor."

"What about your family?" she asked, eager to know more about him.

"I have one sister who lives in Kentucky. She's married with two girls, thirteen and sixteen. My parents live in Chattanooga and try to visit us as often as they can. They both work for the state and hope to retire in the next five years. Then they promise to spend lots of time with us. When they visit, they always come down together. They're very close and have a wonderful marriage," he said, looking more thoughtful than ever.

In the silence that followed, so many questions flooded Mary Kate's mind, one of the main ones being: *How happy was your marriage?* She had heard conflicting rumors but doubted if she would ever know the truth, unless he chose to tell her. That was far from likely. She would probably never talk with him again after this token dinner to show his appreciation.

He was looking at her again, and she found herself shifting nervously beneath his forthright gaze. Despite her efforts to appear nonchalant about Blake Taylor, she could not remain indifferent each time his penetrating blue gaze held hers.

She turned her attention to the coffee, enjoying its taste. No doubt, this was one of those specialty coffees made from fresh beans and ground daily by Sue, the devoted housekeeper.

"Well," she said, looking back at him. "Tell me about your work."

This was always a good, safe subject, she had learned in her years of interviewing. Most people talked easily about their work, even when they detested their job—which Mary Kate secretly found amusing.

He took a deep breath and his tense features visibly relaxed. "My latest project is a special little shopping center near Destin. The design reflects the ocean motif, lots of driftwood, seashells, that sort of thing. It's kind of fun to plan."

"Oh, that does sound like fun. Have you begun work on it?"

"As a matter of fact, we're still in the planning stages, which is one of the reasons I had gone to my beach house near there. Of course, I needed to relax, but I also wanted to go over some of the plans and think about the best way to design the shopping center."

"I see," she nodded. So his trip hadn't been entirely selfish, escaping press and his little daughter. He was attempting to mix business with pleasure.

"Maybe you'd like to come down with me sometime. There's a wonderful restaurant nearby. I could show you what we're doing."

The invitation took Mary Kate totally by surprise. Her first thought was: *Why is he asking me? He's fulfilled his obligation.* Then her next thought was *Whatever the reason, I'd like to go.*

Belatedly, she thought she saw the wisdom of his plan. "Would you want me to do some sort of interview for promotion?"

He groaned. "No, please. I've had more than my share of

press lately. It's the last thing I want." He drained his coffee cup and placed it on the coffee table. "No, my reason for asking you was purely selfish," he said, glancing across at her. "I thought it would be fun to get away from here and get to know you better. You're a very interesting young lady."

She swallowed, trying to take the compliment in stride. "Thank you," she said at length.

"I'm sorry about Hanna's behavior tonight," he turned to her, his full lips drawn in a tight, worried line.

She shifted, propping her elbow against a soft pillow. "Please don't apologize. I can understand how difficult it must be trying to raise a little girl alone—" she broke off, noting the guarded look on his face. Had she said too much?

"We've managed," he said, his tone more formal now. "There haven't been any serious problems—until this trial." His words were heavily underscored, reminding Mary Kate of her own dismal role in publicizing the trial.

She didn't know how to respond. She took a deep breath and tried again. "I just meant I appreciate the problems both of you must have had adjusting to the loss of your wife."

After speaking those words, she could have bitten her tongue off. She watched the handsome face harden to a mask of bitterness. *How could I have become so personal with him in these past minutes when all I wanted was to express concern?* She had assumed enough time had elapsed since Charlotte Taylor's death to allow a gentle reference to her, but Blake's tormented face shouted the truth into the sudden, tense silence.

Somewhere behind them she could hear the tick of a clock as the silence stretched between them. She glanced around the room then met his eyes once again. "Well, I have to be at work early in the morning, and I expect you do, as well. I hope you and Hanna get everything straightened out." It was an innocent remark on her part, but again he seemed to be on the defensive.

"We'll get everything straightened out," he assured her. "But I'm afraid that you're leaving with the impression that our situation is worse than it really is."

"Oh, no, I didn't mean it that way. And I certainly don't want to pry. But I was just wondering. . ."

"What were you wondering?" he asked, studying her curiously.

She cleared her throat. "It might help if Hanna had some counseling, and I know a wonderful Christian counselor."

His brown brows arched questioningly. "Are you saying you think Hanna needs to see a psychiatrist?" The blue eyes darkened and again there was a tightness about his mouth.

"Lots of children see counselors nowadays," Mary Kate answered gently. "Sometimes an outsider who is trained to deal with family problems can accomplish more than a parent who may have become overprotective or—"

"Overworked! I know that's on the tip of your tongue, so I'll say it for you. Yes, I'm overworked. And yes, I should have taken her to the beach with me the day she begged to go. But I needed the time to myself."

"I wasn't about to say anything like that," Mary Kate said, suddenly angered by his quick assumptions.

The sudden silence that filled the room was charged with the electrical tension of strong emotions held in check.

"I must go," she said, reaching for her bag. "Thanks for inviting me."

He hesitated for a moment, almost as though he wanted her to stay, but then he shoved his hands in his pockets and shrugged his broad shoulders lightly. "Thanks for coming," he said, his tone changed.

She sensed that he was sorry for bristling at her remark and she regretted almost snapping at him, but at least the evening was almost over and she wouldn't have to see him again.

"I imagine everything will straighten out in time," she said, feeling awkward now.

He walked her to the door, saying nothing more until they had crossed the foyer. Then as he opened the door for her, he looked at her with a question in his eyes. "You never did respond to my invitation for dinner at the beach. What do you think?"

In view of the tense exchange that had just passed between them, she knew he was only being polite, and she had no desire to go now, anyway.

"I'm sorry. I don't think I'll be able to go."

He nodded, as though he had read her thoughts clearly. "Then again, thanks for trying to help with Hanna."

"No problem." She stepped out onto the porch, momentarily taking in the elegance of the neighborhood—and the loneliness. She turned back. "Thanks for dinner."

"My pleasure. Shall I walk you to the car?" He was looking at her as though he wanted to make up for their argument, but she decided this was a good way to end it.

"I'll be fine," she said, then turned quickly and hurried down the steps and across the sidewalk, her heels clicking loudly in the silence of the summer night. He was still watching her as she backed her car out of the drive and pulled away.

six

The desk phone shattered Mary Kate's quiet concentration as she studied the script for her next interview.

"Not again," she moaned, wondering as she lifted the phone how many times she had been interrupted in the past hour.

"I decided I want to go to Sea World, after all," came a small voice.

Mary Kate had almost forgotten the rumpled tickets in her purse. She blinked, prodding her work-numbed brain a couple of times before she could translate the words and the unspoken plea behind them.

"Hanna, is that you?" she frowned, staring at the mountain of work overflowing her desk.

"Yes. Can we go? Please?"

Mary Kate bit the inside of her lip, recalling her decision to stay out of the Taylors' life after leaving their house two nights ago. And yet, how could she say no to the lonely little voice on the other end of the line?

"Well," she swallowed, closing her eyes to her workload, "if you want to go to Sea World. . .sure, we'll go. When would you like to do that?"

"I could go this weekend," Hanna quickly replied. "I don't have anything to do."

This weekend, Mary Kate thought, recalling how she had planned to collapse on her sofa on Saturday and enjoy the luxury of doing absolutely nothing. Her first day off in weeks.

"Sue already said I could go," Hanna said, as though pleading her case. "Besides, Dad has to go check on one of his projects."

"Okay," Mary Kate heard herself relenting. "I think there's an afternoon show of Shamu around two. How does that sound?"

"Great!" There was no mistaking the excitement in her voice. She sounded like a completely different child than the sullen one Mary Kate had encountered only two nights ago.

"Okay," Mary Kate replied, picking up the child's excitement. "How about if I pick you up at noon? Maybe we could have a pizza first."

"I'll be ready," Hanna answered excitedly. "And thank you," she added quietly.

"You're welcome. Thank you for calling me."

After she hung up, she sat staring at the phone. She couldn't resist the surge of happiness that flowed through her. It made her feel so good to do something kind for Hanna. There was such a sadness about her and her father, and she was sure it stemmed from the tragedy of losing their beautiful mother and wife.

She leaned back in the chair, her thoughts wandering toward Blake Taylor again. What would his reaction be to his daughter going to Sea World with Mary Kate? Of course he wouldn't mind. He would probably be relieved that someone was entertaining his daughter. That thought brought a wave of disappointment to her. Blake Taylor had a lot to learn about being a father. He should have been spending Saturday with his daughter after what had happened this week. Instead, he was off to one of his projects. When was the man going to learn?

"The dolphins were so cute, weren't they?" Hanna asked, beaming up at Mary Kate.

Steering the car into the slower lane of traffic, Mary Kate stole a glance at her little friend. Her blond hair was combed neatly in place, and she was wearing a blue, two-piece outfit that looked as though it had come from a very expensive children's shop. She smiled at Hanna.

It had been a delightful Saturday for both Mary Kate and Hanna. Mary Kate had joined in the fun with Hanna, telling her stories about her own childhood over pizza as Hanna listened intently, a strange look on her face. It occurred to Mary Kate that Hanna had missed out on so much in her life, specifically a normal childhood. Later, as they sat together, munching popcorn, taking in the antics of the animals at Sea World, Hanna had squealed with delight.

Glancing down at the little girl whose blue eyes glowed with excitement, Mary Kate felt happier than she had felt in a long time. It warmed her heart to see Hanna having such a good time. What, she wondered, did the child normally do on Saturday? From their conversation, she didn't seem to have many friends, and Mary Kate wondered about that, although she had refrained from asking personal questions.

"We'll spend another Saturday together sometime if you'd like to."

"I would." Hanna was studying her strangely. "Can I come to see you sometime?"

"You want to come to my junked-up place?" Mary Kate laughed. "Well, sure. But I'll have to warn you, I'm not a good housekeeper."

"Mother wasn't either," Hanna said, turning her eyes back to the road. "Sue did all the work." Then her eyes lit up again as she turned to Mary Kate. "Maybe Sue could come over and help you out."

"Oh, I don't think I could afford Sue," Mary Kate said, turning into Hanna's neighborhood. "And besides, she's needed at your house."

"Yeah, but she gets bored. She runs out of things to do."

"She does?" Mary Kate glanced at her, thinking it should be a busy life, taking care of Hanna and her father, doing the housework and the cooking.

"She has a cleaning woman who comes in twice a week to help out. And she orders meals from a take-out shop lots of evenings. And sometimes Dad and I eat out."

"Oh, you do?" Mary Kate asked with interest, thinking maybe she had been a bit hard on Hanna's father, after all.

"Yes, he lets me choose a restaurant and we go out once a week. I like tacos," she smiled at Mary Kate who nodded in agreement.

"What else do you do?" she asked, wanting to know more.

"I sometimes go to visit my mother's parents in Memphis."

"Do you have fun?" Mary Kate asked hopefully, although she already suspected she knew the answer judging from the child's sad face.

"Not anymore. All Grandmother wants to do is talk about Mother. And she cries a lot."

Mary Kate nodded. That was exactly the sort of thing Hanna didn't need.

"Mother was an only child, so I don't even have cousins to play with."

"What about your dad's parents?"

Her eyes lit up. "I do have fun when I go to see Grandma and Grandpa. They live in Chattanooga."

"Do you have cousins on your dad's side?"

Hanna giggled. "Rachel and Tina. They're teenagers and they're always talking about dating." She giggled. "When I visit them, they let me play dress-up with their things, and they take me to movies and shopping."

"That sounds like fun. Where do they live?'

"In Kentucky," she sighed. "So I don't get to go there very often."

Mary Kate nodded sagely as she turned into the drive. It occurred to her that Hanna was probably the loneliest little girl she had ever met. She wondered why she didn't have more friends, and she decided it was time to come right out and ask.

"Do you have many friends in your neighborhood?"

Hanna sighed. "Not anymore. I used to have friends, but then when Mother was sick, I couldn't have company, and then..." her voice trailed away.

"You could have company now, couldn't you?" Mary Kate frowned at her, thinking something was terribly amiss here. It was bad enough that she had lost her mother, now she seemed to have lost her friends as well.

"I don't want to play with them," she answered defiantly.

Mary Kate stared at her. "Why not?"

Something in her face closed down, and Mary Kate realized she was not going to get an answer to her question.

"I just don't," she said, reaching for the door handle. "Thanks for taking me." Her voice was more formal now, and Mary Kate realized with a pang of sadness that the questions she had asked had put a gap in their friendship. She so wanted to return to the warm, funny state they had shared earlier, but she had no idea how.

"Hey," she said, reaching across the seat to touch Hanna's

arm, "if you like tacos, do you like spaghetti?"

Hanna looked surprised by the question. Then, thinking it over, she began to nod. "I like spaghetti."

"Then you're in luck. It's the only thing I cook decently. Want to come over sometime and help me make spaghetti? We might even make cookies afterwards."

Hanna's blue eyes lit up again. "When?"

Mary Kate mentally ran her hectic week through her mind and hit a wall. "Why don't I call you? I'd say tomorrow, but I've already promised my Sunday school class I'd go to lunch with them." Then another idea came to her. "Do you go to Sunday school, Hanna?"

She shook her head. "I go to church when I visit Grandma in Chattanooga."

Mary Kate nodded, making a mental note to do something about that.

"Why don't I call you about that spaghetti?" Mary Kate winked at her.

"Okay." Hanna pushed open the door and hopped out, smiling back at Mary Kate. "Thanks." She slammed the door and skipped, swinging her bag of souvenirs, up to the front door where Sue was waiting. She waved to Mary Kate who waved back before leaving.

All the way home, she kept thinking about what an enchanting little girl Hanna was. She would be so easy to love, but she couldn't get involved. *Why not?* A voice in her head questioned.

Because getting involved with Hanna might mean getting involved with her dad, and Mary Kate knew she had to avoid that. *Perhaps one more outing with Hanna wouldn't hurt anything,* she reasoned, humming to herself as she drove home.

ᘔ

The first part of Mary Kate's week was as hectic as usual, and by Tuesday night she was exhausted. She had already taken her bath, jumped into her comfortable pajamas, and settled down on the sofa with a bag of popcorn when the telephone rang, intruding on her favorite television program.

With a sigh of resignation, she placed the popcorn on the table and reached for the phone. "Hello," she tried to sound more pleasant than she felt.

"Mary Kate?"

She bolted to attention, knowing instinctively that the voice on the other end belonged to Blake Taylor.

"Yes?" She tried to control a ridiculous leap of her heart as she waited for him to continue.

"This is Blake Taylor. I wanted to thank you for taking Hanna to Sea World on Saturday. She had a wonderful time. She's still talking about the dolphins."

Mary Kate smiled, remembering. "Strange that you should call. I was thinking about phoning to see if she could come over for spaghetti on Thursday evening. We sort of discussed doing that."

"Sounds like a good idea, if she isn't overloaded with homework."

"I promise to have her home by seven-thirty," Mary Kate said, wondering why she sounded apologetic.

There was a moment's hesitation, and it occurred to Mary Kate that he might enjoy joining them, but she just wasn't up to another jolting encounter with Blake Taylor so she kept silent.

"I'll mention this to Hanna if you like."

"Yes, would you please?"

"Sure. Hold on a minute."

She could hear the phone being placed on something solid, then steps retreated over a tiled floor. He must be on the kitchen phone, she deduced, since it was the only area of the house that was not plushly carpeted. In a matter of seconds, he was back.

"She's thrilled. Shall I drop her off?"

"Er no," she answered quickly, then bit her tongue. "I'm not sure just what time I'll be getting away from the station. What would work best for me is to pick her up after I leave work. I'd say that will be around six, but I'll call first."

"Fine. I'll tell her. Well," he hesitated for a moment, "thanks again for what you're doing for her."

"Believe me, I'm having as much fun as she. Maybe more," she added, realizing that this was really true.

"Have a good week," he said before hanging up.

After she replaced the phone, she sat staring into space, trying to analyze her reasons for avoiding Blake. His reputation? There was still some buzz about the jewelry incident, and she had a feeling Brad wouldn't want her seeing him. He would make noises about her "image." But that wasn't really it, she knew in her heart of hearts. The man had a strange effect on her. The truth was, she didn't quite know how to react to him. He was older, more sophisticated, and he had been married to a woman who had died a painful death. He must be suffering terribly. She didn't know what to say to him or how to act in that situation. In fact, the whole thing was so complicated that she couldn't begin to sort through her feelings. What confused her most of all was her own response to him. He made her heart beat faster, and brought an odd tingling to her skin, and all the while she felt hot and cold at the same time.

Nerves, she decided, *pure and simple.* And the best cure

was to avoid him completely.

It made perfect sense, she told herself, picking up her popcorn again and trying to catch up on what she had missed of her TV show. To her disappointment, she had lost interest in television, and now her mind kept straying to Blake.

Disgusted, she got up and went to the kitchen to make herself a cup of hot chocolate. *I'm just over-tired from the past two strenuous days. A cup of hot chocolate, early to bed, my nightly devotion, and maybe I'll flip through my Bible—that's what I need.* She needed some peace of mind and in the last hour, it seemed to have fled. Blake's call had left her rattled.

As she waited for the hot chocolate to warm in the microwave, she thought again of what Hanna had said about church. She only went with her grandmother. No wonder the poor little girl was at a loss. She couldn't believe Blake had neglected taking her to church. Surely her mother had, before she became ill.

The bell on the microwave rang, and she opened the door, pondering the thought of inviting Hanna to go to church with her. It seemed like the least she could do. In fact, that was far more important than taking her to Sea World or cooking spaghetti for her.

She suddenly felt better as she headed toward her bedroom, sipping her hot chocolate. She had made a decision and she knew she was doing the right thing.

≈

On Thursday evening when Mary Kate pulled into the Taylor driveway to pick up Hanna, she saw a black European import parked in the driveway. Blake Taylor was already home. She had hoped to avoid him, but now there seemed to be no chance of that. Maybe Hanna would be ready and waiting at the door. Resisting the impulse to merely blow the horn, she got out of the car and hurried up to knock on the front door.

Immediately it swung back and she was staring into Blake's deep blue eyes. "Good evening," he said with a little smile. His business suit was rumpled, his tie loosened. The blue eyes were weary, haggard, underlined with dark circles. Mary Kate thought he must work very hard, or perhaps he pushed himself deeper in his work to escape his problems.

She glanced over his shoulder, searching for the little girl.

"Hi. Is Hanna ready? I'm running a bit late."

"No time for a quick cup of coffee?"

She shook her head. "Afraid not."

Quick little steps sounded behind him and the little girl pushed around her father, a wide smile on her face.

"Hi," she said, smiling at Mary Kate. She was wearing jeans and the T-shirt she had bought at Sea World on Saturday. Her blond hair was neatly combed and her face looked as though it had just been scrubbed.

"Hi, Hanna. Ready to go?"

She bolted forward as her dad's hand shot to her shoulder. "Not even a good-bye?" he asked, looking at her with sad eyes.

"Bye, Dad." As he knelt down, she gave him a quick kiss on the cheek, and Mary Kate felt a warm tenderness tugging at her heart.

"I'll have her back by seven-thirty, as I promised," Mary Kate said as Hanna tugged at her hand and they turned to go.

"Have fun," he called after them.

"Thanks," Mary Kate waved.

Several thoughts concerning Blake were bouncing around in her head, but Mary Kate vowed to sort them out later. Hanna yanked open her car door and leapt into the front seat, as though this was already a familiar routine.

❧

The next hour flew by at Mary Kate's place. While Mary Kate prepared the spaghetti, Hanna played with Bo on the living room floor.

The living room–dining area flowed into the kitchen and it was easy to peer around a corner to keep an eye on Hanna. Bo, the black cocker spaniel, had become hyper with his new playmate. He had Hanna down on the floor, licking her right in the face. Mary Kate could imagine Blake Taylor's reaction to this scene.

"Bo, stop that!" Mary Kate scolded, although Hanna was squealing with laughter.

Mary Kate hurried to the hall closet to get out a small plastic bucket of his toys. "He likes to play fetch. Maybe if you gently toss the rubber ball, he'll play fetch with you." She turned to Bo and pointed a finger as he wagged his tail happily. "Now, you settle down; otherwise, you'll have to spend some time in the bathroom with the door closed."

He merely licked her hand good-naturedly, too thrilled with his new playmate to be bothered by a little scolding from his mistress.

Mary Kate hurried back to the kitchen just in time to grab the pan of pasta before the water boiled over onto the stove. Lowering the heat, she replaced the pan and turned to pick up a wooden spoon. She was eager to sample the sauce. Her lunch had consisted of an apple, a box of raisins, and a container of juice—all devoured on the run. In fact, she rarely sat down for a relaxed meal. She had to slow down and start leading a sensible life, like she assumed other people did.

When the sauce and pasta were almost ready, she turned to the cabinet and reached for two bright red plates and placed them on the counter. She lived very casually and didn't plan to alter her lifestyle one bit. She opened the silverware drawer, pulled out two stainless steel place settings, then reached into the refrigerator for the salad she had put together the night before. She uncovered the plastic container and placed it on the counter. Now she added salad bowls and dressing to the counter and peered back at Hanna.

"You want milk to drink, Hanna?"

She was squealing with delight as Bo loped back to her side, the ball in his mouth.

"Milk?" she repeated louder.

"I don't like milk," she glanced at Mary Kate.

"Oh? What do you usually drink at dinner?"

"Cola. Or root beer."

Mary Kate frowned. "Sorry, I don't have either one. How about chocolate milk?"

Hanna shrugged. "Maybe."

Mary Kate took that as yes and prepared it for her, adding an extra scoop of chocolate powder to entice the little girl. *Didn't her father mind her not drinking milk?* she wondered. Again, she assumed Blake Taylor was too busy with his career to keep a proper eye on his daughter. *And what was Sue thinking?* She wondered about that for a moment, then realized it was probably easier to give in to Hanna than to discipline her, which was always a mistake.

"Okay, come get it," she called, reminding herself this was not her child to raise, and she should keep her nose out of the Taylors' business.

Hanna ate heartily, turning to offer Bo a bite of spaghetti.

"Please don't do that, Hanna," Mary Kate spoke firmly. "I feed him in his bowl in the kitchen after meals."

For a moment, Hanna looked as though she would rebel.

"I'll let you put his food together later. Okay?"

Hanna smiled, satisfied with the compromise.

The evening went well, and Mary Kate couldn't believe it was already seven o'clock by the time they finished the meal and played with Bo.

"Hanna, look at the time," she pointed. "I promised your dad I'd have you home by seven-thirty."

All the joy drained from her little girl's face. "I don't want to go home," she pouted.

"Then that will give us an excuse to do this again."

"But you promised we would bake cookies."

Mary Kate took a deep breath, wishing she hadn't been so enthusiastic with her invitation. "Well, we'll do that next time."

"You're breaking your promise again," Hanna's blue eyes darkened as her mouth turned downward.

Mary Kate studied her face and wondered how often she used this ploy to get her way, even though she had a valid point.

"Either I have to break my promise to you or to your dad. Since your dad is the boss for both of us on this, if I break my promise to him you might not get to come back. And Bo and I want you to come back again. So, now can we agree on that?"

Hanna chewed the inside of her lip, and Mary Kate could see the mental wheels turning. "I guess so," she shrugged, turning to give Bo a last hug.

Finally, they were out the door and into the car, heading back home. Hanna was in good spirits again, chatting happily about Bo.

A thought kept nagging at Mary Kate. Another Sunday was coming up and she wouldn't mind picking Hanna up for Sunday school. It seemed such a waste for her not to attend church.

Don't get involved, a voice warned. But as a Christian, she couldn't help thinking God had put this child in her life for a reason. She felt strongly that one reason was to see that she got in church. If Mary Kate didn't invite her, who would?

She took a deep breath and plunged in. "Hanna, how would you like to come to Sunday school with me on Sunday? Last week they were talking about the puppet show they were having this Sunday. I think you'd enjoy that."

"A puppet show?" she swung around on the car seat, her eyes wide. "Why would they have a puppet show in a *church?*"

The lights of a passing car flashed over them, and above the muted lights of her dashboard, Mary Kate saw the doubt in Hanna's eyes.

"Well, you see, the teachers use puppets to tell Bible stories. It's a lot of fun. I think you'd enjoy it, really. Want me to come pick you up Sunday morning?"

"Maybe," she nodded, squirming. "I like puppets."

"Great." Then she hesitated, realizing she hadn't even mentioned this to Hanna's father. "I'll ask your dad about it when we get home." She tried to suppress the heavy sigh that was building in her chest. She dreaded another encounter with him, and yet she knew that getting Hanna in Sunday school where she would be surrounded by caring adults and friendly children would be worth the effort.

She turned into the driveway, and as her car lights swept over the sprawling Spanish home, the front door was already swinging open.

He was dressed in jeans and a T-shirt, and seeing him in a more relaxed manner made Mary Kate more cautious than ever. It was easier to think of him as the super businessman with whom she had little in common when he was in business clothes. Seeing him in comfortable clothes and smiling, as he was now, made her want to be friends with him. And she couldn't be.

"Hello," he called to them.

"Dad, you should see Bo."

"Bo?" His blue eyes held a question as he looked from Hanna to Mary Kate.

"My cocker spaniel," Mary Kate explained.

"Oh."

Why did he look relieved? Mary Kate wondered. *Did he think Bo was her boyfriend and that she had made her meal with Hanna a threesome?*

"Won't you come in?" he asked Mary Kate.

He looked more friendly than before as he glanced from Hanna who was smiling happily at him, back to Mary Kate. Even though she knew the man had no interest in her beyond his daughter's friendship, Mary Kate felt unsettled by his good looks and the intense blue gaze in his eyes.

"I have to go. Thanks anyway." She hesitated, glancing down at Hanna. "Bye."

"Bye. See you Sunday," Hanna called over her shoulder as she disappeared into the house.

"Sunday?" Blake looked back at Mary Kate.

She caught her breath. In the confusion, she had forgotten to ask his permission. She cleared her throat. "Would you mind if I took Hanna to Sunday school?"

He stared at her for a moment then his eyes moved on to something in the darkness. "I've already made plans for the two of us," he said, his tone more formal now.

Mary Kate realized she had struck a nerve with him but failed to see why.

"Well, maybe some other time," she suggested.

When he did not acknowledge the offer with further comment, Mary Kate was scarcely able to hide her irritation. She had a strong urge to tell him just what she thought of his method of child rearing. She couldn't do that. After all, it was none of her business. There seemed to be nothing more to say so she turned to go.

His hand reached out, gripping her arm. The warm strength of his fingers brought a catch to her throat and she whirled back to him, her brows lifted questioningly.

"Thank you for entertaining Hanna this evening," he said, suddenly releasing her. He seemed to regret having touched her. It was as though he reacted before he thought. They were both silent for a moment, causing her to linger just when she would have pulled away.

Mary Kate didn't like the way she felt drawn toward him, wanting to stay and talk. But she had to keep her distance. "You're welcome," she replied. This time she was the one whose tone was formal. "Good night," she said, hurrying down the steps.

As she walked quickly to her car, she tried to figure the man out. What went on inside that complicated brain of his? His voice told her one thing, while his eyes, his touch, revealed something else entirely.

As she drove back to her apartment, Mary Kate couldn't stop thinking about him. She even rubbed her arm gently, where his fingers had rested. Her experience with romance had been limited to a high school boyfriend who was really just a friend, and several dates in college. There had been a brief fascination or two, but she had never been in love. Her mother had told her she was too picky, but the truth was she kept waiting for that special magic she saw between her parents. She had always thought she might prefer someone older, but she dared not consider Blake Taylor a possibility.

He had been married with a child. And there was still a cloud over his head concerning the jewelry theft. No, she couldn't feel anything for the man even though the love song on the radio stirred a deep longing in her soul.

She pondered the tension between Blake and her. Strong vibrations crackled in the air when they were in the same room, so that, inevitably, they ended up snapping at each other or glaring silently, unable to speak at all.

It was just too bewildering to figure out.

&

As Mary Kate unlocked her door and flipped on the lights, Bo came running to meet her. It was good to have someone waiting for her when she came home at night, even if it was only her beloved little dog.

"You've had quite a night, haven't you?" she teased him.

Glancing around, she heaved a sigh at the disorder of her duplex. She had moved in, months before, with the idea of completely renovating the plain rooms. But there had been no time.

"Oh well," she turned to Bo and shook her head, "you don't really mind, do you?"

She reached down to stroke his soft fur and they both wandered back to her bedroom. She wanted a relaxing soak in the tub and then she was going to jump into bed and read for a while.

As she passed the dresser mirror, she hesitated, studying her reflection. She had changed into jeans and an oversized white blouse after she and Hanna came back, and she noted that the white accented the darkness of her hair and eyes. She found herself wondering what Blake thought of her, as she appraised her petite reflection. She had narrow shoulders, a tiny waist, flaring hips, and legs that were too long for her small frame—attractive, but definitely not the figure of a model.

She turned and moved on into the bathroom, thinking of that relaxing soak in the tub that she had promised herself. Nothing soothed her nerves like lounging in the tub surrounded with bubbles and scented oil.

Suddenly, the phone jangled on the nightstand in the bedroom. She glanced at her watch. Eight o'clock. This had better not be some ridiculous night assignment Brad was asking her to do at this hour. She hurried back into the bedroom and grabbed the ringing phone.

To her surprise, it was Blake Taylor's voice on the other end of the wire.

"Mary Kate, am I disturbing you?" he asked politely.

"No—" *Why is* he *calling?* she wondered, fighting a burst of excitement at the sound of his voice.

He cleared his throat. "Hanna's really disappointed about missing that puppet show on Sunday," he said. "So I've canceled our plans. If you still would like her to go, I don't object."

Object? Thank you very much, she was tempted to respond. He should be pleased she was making the effort to take his daughter to church, when he didn't take her himself.

"Fine," she said, matter-of-factly. "I'll pick her up at nine-thirty. My church is only fifteen minutes from your house, and Sunday school starts at a quarter of ten."

"She'll be ready," he said quietly.

Mary Kate sensed that he wanted to say more, but she didn't give him time.

"Tell her I'll see her then. Thanks for letting her go."

"Thanks for taking her—"

"Good night," she said quickly, scarcely hearing his reply before she hung up.

She was on the brink of being rude to him, but she couldn't help it. The man unnerved her, and she knew she had to keep a tight rein on this situation. In fact, it might be a good idea if she didn't continue to see Hanna, she decided, going into the bathroom to run water in the tub. Maybe getting her started in Sunday school would influence her father to take her, and Mary Kate could drop her role as companion.

The situation was a difficult one, at best. First, she had put Blake on guard in that awful interview. Then he had interpreted her concern for Hanna as criticism of his parenting, and now she was stealing valuable time he had planned to spend with his daughter.

She sighed, opening the cabinet for a towel and washcloth. She would miss being with Hanna. The little girl was winning her heart, she thought, reaching for the bath oil.

God, how am I going to handle this? she silently prayed.

seven

"Those puppets were really neat!" Hanna exclaimed, her blue eyes dancing as Mary Kate steered the car out of the church parking lot. "I never had so much fun in Sunday school."

Mary Kate glanced across at her and smiled. She looked so cute today, wearing a pink dress with a Peter Pan collar and delicate pearl buttons down the front. She wore black patent leather shoes and had a tiny matching purse on her arm.

"Thank you, Hanna. Glad you had a good time. Did you pick out that pretty dress?"

Her eyes darkened as she looked away. "No, Mommy bought it before she got so sick."

The words ripped through Mary Kate's heart. It wasn't the first time Hanna had referred to her mother, and now she could see the pain on the little girl's face. She bit her lip, trying to think what to say. Should she change the subject or encourage Hanna to talk about her mother? She had no idea what to do, but then Hanna solved the problem.

"Mommy's in heaven," she said, turning on the seat to look at Mary Kate. "Grandma told me that at the hospital."

Mary Kate swallowed hard, shaking her head. "That's right. And you'll see her again some day."

"Grandma says I need to give my heart to Jesus. How do I do that?"

Mary Kate was grateful for the red light, giving her a chance to slow down and gather her thoughts. "Would you like to talk to my pastor sometime, Hanna? Or even your

Sunday school teacher might be better at explaining it that I am. But I can tell you what I did."

"What did you do?" Hanna turned her head, studying Mary Kate thoughtfully.

Mary Kate thought back to her childhood and the small country church she had loved so much. "Come to think of it, I was exactly your age. Eight years old. It was the Sunday after Bible school, the first week in June—June 7th, as a matter of fact. I had been learning about becoming a Christian during Bible school. My teacher told me that all I had to do was confess my sins and believe that Jesus came down to earth to die for those sins. I believed that then and I believe it now. So I walked down the aisle on Sunday morning when the altar call was given and told the pastor what I had decided." She glanced at Hanna. "I remember feeling so happy that day, and it still makes me happy to think about becoming a Christian."

Hanna was quiet for a moment, staring at Mary Kate. Then she sank back against the seat and stared out the window. Mary Kate imagined she was thinking this over; maybe even now she was feeling a tug on her heart to do the very same thing.

"Can I come back with you next Sunday?" Hanna looked at her.

Mary Kate remembered her vow not to get further involved after today, but now she knew she had no choice. If she could help Hanna to become a Christian, it would be one of the most wonderful things that could happen.

"Of course," she said tenderly.

The light had changed and as they drove into Hanna's neighborhood, Mary Kate thought perhaps Hanna could influence her father to come to church. The thought of Hanna's father drew Mary Kate's eyes to the rearview mirror, assessing her image. She had worn a blue linen suit with short sleeves and a blue floral scarf tucked into the open collar. Her dark hair was shining from the morning's shampoo and her eyes sparkled with happiness. She always felt better after going to church.

Her eyes darted back to the street, to the Taylor house they were now approaching. She turned into the driveway and stopped the car.

"Well—"

"Aren't you coming in?" Hanna whirled, her eyes wide.

"I can't, honey. Sorry."

Then, looking over Hanna's head to the front yard, she spotted Blake walking toward them. He was dressed in casual clothes, and for once he looked relaxed and rested. He opened the car door for Hanna.

"Dad, the puppet show was great!" she said, hopping out of the car. "But Mary Kate won't come in."

Mary Kate noted the little pout forming on Hanna's mouth and knew instantly that she had her own methods for getting her way with her dad.

"Do you have to go?" Blake, too, looked disappointed, but Mary Kate tried not to think about that.

"Yes, I do."

"Are you sure? We hoped you would stay for lunch."

She sighed. "I really can't. I'm sorry, but thanks anyway."

Blake turned to Hanna. "Run get your play clothes on. I thought we'd ride over to the beach if you want to."

"Yippee," Hanna yelled, darting across the yard, her pink skirt flying.

Blake opened the door wider. "May I talk with you for a moment?"

Mary Kate swallowed. "Sure." She stretched one arm across the steering wheel and moved her purse over with the other as Blake sat down.

"I hope you know how much I appreciate your kindness to Hanna. I was hoping you'd have lunch with us and then go to our beach house for the afternoon. I should have asked sooner. Sorry."

"That's okay," she answered quickly, trying not to look into his blue eyes. He was so handsome and so appealing when he spoke in that soft rich tone. It was becoming more difficult for her not to feel a strong attraction to him.

There was a genuine humility in his voice that drew her attention to his face. The brown hair and brows were offset by the rich blue of his eyes, and the hard line of jaw and chin were somehow softened by the quiet pleading in his level gaze.

She dragged her eyes away and tapped her fingers on the steering wheel. "Well," she began, trying to assemble her thoughts—before she made an excuse. She was suddenly thinking of Hanna's expression of concern about becoming a Christian. How could she hold grudges against Blake Taylor? As a Christian she wasn't supposed to do that, and she knew it.

"You probably noticed I was a bit sensitive about church," he said, breaking into her thoughts. "That's one more area I need to work on. When Charlotte died so young, I had trouble accepting that as God's will, in my mother's words. My mother believes that everything is in God's hands, and I guess I didn't want to see it that way. In any case," he sighed, "Hanna needs to be in church and I want to thank you again for taking her."

"You're welcome," she said gently. Maybe she had judged

him too harshly, after all. She was about to say as much but his next words threw her completely off guard.

"Is there some reason you want to avoid being with me?" he asked directly.

She caught her breath, startled by his frankness. Her eyes flew to his face and she looked him directly in the eyes, wanting to say the right thing. When she realized he was staring at her, too, she turned and focused on the clean white lines of the Spanish-style house.

"No, of course not," she answered nervously.

"There's something else I'd like to say." He took a deep breath as though whatever he wanted to say was difficult.

Mary Kate waited, holding her breath. Tension crackled between them like electricity and her stomach was knotting.

"I would like for you to know," he turned back to her, his blue eyes suddenly vulnerable, "that I am not a thief. I was innocent of the charges against me."

Mary Kate felt a blush creeping up her cheeks, and she realized with a sinking heart, that he knew this was one of the reasons she had been avoiding him.

"I'd also like for you to know that I have not asked another woman out since. . .my wife died."

Mary Kate looked into his face and felt her heart melt. All her defenses tumbled and she knew she was lost. There was no way she could keep on saying no to him.

"I'm honored that you chose to invite me," she said quietly. "And I never thought you guilty of those charges."

There, it was out in the open now. He heaved a deep sigh, as a wide smile flashed over his face. "Thank God."

Mary Kate's eyes drifted toward the house as she thought about the empty afternoon stretching before her. Why not accept his invitation, after all? There was nothing she'd rather do than spend a Sunday afternoon with Hanna and Blake.

"Tell you what," she said with a smile. "I need to go home and see about Bo, and I want to change into something more comfortable. Then I really would like to ride over to the beach with you and Hanna."

There was no mistaking the look of pleasure on his face. "That's marvelous. What time should we pick you up?"

"In an hour?" she asked, glancing at her watch.

"That's perfect. Thanks for changing your mind."

Her brown eyes locked with his and for a moment, neither spoke. Then, awkwardly, she turned in her seat and focused on the key in the ignition. "I'd better get going, then," she said, turning the key. "By the way, what if I pack us a little picnic snack?"

"Sounds great. I'll tell Hanna you're coming," he called cheerfully as he got out of the car.

Waving, she backed out of the driveway and drove off, thinking about her afternoon with Blake and Hanna.

≈

An hour later she was surprised to see a white sport utility vehicle pulling into her driveway when she was expecting the black luxury sports sedan she had seen in Blake's drive. But there was no doubt it was Blake and Hanna. Hanna's face was pressed to the car window, and her eyes were wide with anticipation as Mary Kate hurried out and locked the front door.

She started toward the backseat when the front door was thrust open. "Where's Bo?" Hanna demanded. "He likes the beach, doesn't he?"

Mary Kate wasn't sure Blake would appreciate black cocker spaniel fur on his upholstery. "Yes, he does, but—"

"Dad, Bo can come too, can't he?"

"Absolutely—I'm outnumbered here." Blake hopped out

and came around the car, taking the picnic basket from Mary Kate's hands.

"Are you sure, Blake? Your upholstery—"

"Positive. I'll put this in the back."

Hanna jumped out of the car, grabbed Mary Kate by the hand, and dragged her to the house to get Bo.

"What's in the picnic basket?" Hanna asked, her eyes dancing with excitement as Mary Kate unlocked the door.

"Just a snack for later." Mary Kate opened the door and called Bo. He bounded out the door to greet Hanna with a wet kiss. Mary Kate turned to see if Blake had changed his mind about taking her wiggling dog along, but the wide grin on his face told her not to worry. He seemed to be enjoying Hanna's giggles of joy as she dodged Bo's wet nose.

Hanna ran for the backseat with Bo on her heels. Bo stopped, waiting for permission from his mistress before he jumped in behind Hanna.

Hopping into the front seat, Mary Kate smiled first at Hanna then at Blake, after he had settled in under the wheel. They were both wearing shorts and T-shirts and looked relaxed and happy. She sighed with relief. It was nice to see both of them looking this way for a change.

"You've never been to our summer place," Hanna said, her eyes twinkling.

Blake laughed. "We call it that even though we go there year-round. But when Hanna is out of school, we're able to spend a lot more time there, so we refer to it as the summer place."

"Well, it sounds great to me," Mary Kate said, buckling the seat belt over her yellow shorts and matching T-shirt.

"You aren't very tan," Hanna said, staring at Mary Kate's legs.

"Hanna," her father scolded softly although Mary Kate only laughed as they drove away from her apartment.

"No, I don't have a summer place, nor do I have much free time to spend at one. I'm afraid Bo and I may get spoiled today, Hanna, once we see what we've been missing."

Hanna giggled and squirmed around in the seat whenever Bo sniffed her ear. Blake was concentrating on the traffic and said nothing as he drove along, but his expression was calm and pleasant, as though he were enjoying himself.

He took the bypass around Seabreeze and soon they were onto the road to Seaside with the other Sunday afternoon traffic.

"Don't you go to the beach on the weekends?" Blake asked casually. "Surely you aren't working then."

"You work a lot of weekends, Dad," Hanna frowned at him in the mirror.

He chuckled. "You're right, I do. But I'm going to be doing less of that now," he looked back at his daughter and winked.

"Since I'm the newest reporter, I get called lots of times to cover assignments because the other reporters have seniority and can get their time off. I really haven't minded, because I don't know that many people here. Sometimes my weekends are lonely—no offense, Bo," she smiled over her shoulder. After she had made that confession, she bit her tongue. She was getting too personal with them; she hated to admit she got lonely, but of course she did.

Blake darted a curious glance at her. "I should think you'd have plenty of invitations," he spoke casually.

She shrugged. "I do, I suppose. Maybe I'm just picky," she laughed, looking at Hanna. "I like being with little girls with big blue eyes and blond hair."

Hanna squealed with laughter. Mary Kate smiled at her,

then glanced over at her father, who looked in the mirror at Hanna and grinned.

"Excited, aren't you?" he teased.

She nodded, glancing back at Mary Kate.

They had reached the first strip of tourist shops that always seemed to entice people from other areas. Hanna showed little interest in the shops that advertised T-shirts, caps, souvenirs, even ice cream and hot dogs. She had pressed her hands on the console between the bucket seats and was staring straight ahead, as though watching for something.

"Are you going to tell me where to turn?" Blake glanced at her.

"It's after that second red light," Hanna answered proudly.

"That's right."

As Mary Kate listened to the exchange between the two, she realized it was probably a familiar game they played each time they came to their summer place, with Hanna giving directions, proud that she knew the way.

At the second light, they turned onto a quieter street with small beach houses and an occasional market or restaurant.

"The next light," she pointed and Blake chuckled.

"Right again."

"No, you turn left," Hanna giggled.

"Can't even trick you!"

As Mary Kate leaned back against the seat and let her eyes drift from father to daughter and back again, she wondered why she had ever worried that Blake Taylor was not a good father. He and his daughter were obviously close, despite the terrible hardship they had been through of losing wife and mother, and then the awful charges of theft and the trial that followed.

She blinked and turned back to the road, feeling really

sorry for both of them. Hanna was jabbering about a little girl she had met at the beach the last time they were here as she scratched Bo behind the ears. Mary Kate wasn't really listening, however; her attention was drawn to the exclusive area they had entered. Nice beach houses sat on spacious lots, overlooking the serene blue water. Mary Kate couldn't help being impressed. At the end of the street, Blake turned into a driveway, and she stared at this house. It was different from the others in that it was an A-shaped house, or chalet, like one would expect to see out west or up in the mountains.

"It's different, isn't it?" he glanced across at Mary Kate.

"I like it," she said while Hanna and Bo squirmed on the seat, eager to get out of the car.

Mary Kate opened the door and stepped aside as Hanna and Bo raced up the little walkway that led to the cozy chalet.

When Hanna was far enough that she couldn't hear, he lowered his voice and explained. "My wife and I enjoyed skiing in Colorado. When we saw this place, we had to buy it, although we would have liked something larger."

At the mention of his deceased wife, Mary Kate felt odd, as though she were trespassing into territory that belonged only to his family. She hesitated, staring at the chalet. Blake seemed to have sensed her sudden reserve because his tone changed to a more casual one.

"Hanna and I come here every chance we get. There's no longer any sadness attached to it."

She turned and met his gaze directly and saw that he did not look sad, merely a bit wistful. She wanted to ask questions about his wife but she knew that was the last thing she needed to do. She had been invited to come for fun, and she owed it to both of them to keep the conversation pleasant and light.

"Well, I can see why you'd come here often. It's wonderful."

They walked up the walk as Blake reached into his pocket and withdrew a key ring. Hanna was already at the door, jumping up and down, impatient to be inside, with Bo waiting at her side.

After Blake unlocked the door and they entered, Mary Kate took in the simple floor plan. It was a typical chalet, with living room, dining room and kitchen all on the main floor and a guest bath. The color scheme was a warm yellow, with white wicker furnishings and lots of colorful paintings. A spiral stairway of black wrought iron wound upward to the loft.

"Let me show you my room," Hanna grabbed her hand and Mary Kate followed.

Up the stairs they went to the loft where two large bedrooms were separated by a huge bath. Hanna's room was decorated in bright blue, and Mary Kate found herself thinking of a summer sky and white clouds, since the furniture was white and the bedspread and curtains were a delicate white eyelet. A small twin-size bed was filled with stuffed animals.

"This is really pretty, Hanna." Mary Kate turned back to the little girl. "I can see why you love coming here. You're very lucky."

Hanna tilted her head and studied her from an angle, and for a moment, Mary Kate wondered if her choice of words had been wrong. Was she so lucky, after all, losing her mother to a terminal illness and her father to his work? But now he seemed to be making a sincere effort to spend time with her.

"Want to walk down to the beach?" Hanna asked.

"Sure, why not?" Mary Kate smiled, as they held hands again and walked down the stairs.

Blake was in the kitchen, checking out the contents of the deep freeze. "We're in luck," he said. "I thought I had left some ground chuck here. Why don't I thaw it out in the microwave and grill hamburgers for us later on?"

"But what about the picnic?" Hanna frowned.

"It's just a snack, really," Mary Kate laughed. "I doubt that it could hold us for long. A hamburger sounds great," she looked back at Blake.

"Dad, we're gonna walk down to the beach, okay?"

"Fine. Here, let me unlock the sliding doors."

Blake hurried out of the kitchen into the living room. At the end wall, he unlatched the doors, admitting the fresh sea breeze. As they stepped out onto the deck, Mary Kate's eyes made a sweep of the broad beach and the gentle waves lapping into the shoreline. She sighed.

"Hanna, thanks for inviting me," she said, squeezing the little girl's hand.

"We have to leave our shoes here on the porch and go barefoot. Then we can wash our feet over there when we come back." She pointed to a water faucet, placed conveniently near the steps. It was a comfortable, beautiful place, and Blake seemed to have thought of everything.

Mary Kate and Hanna spent the next hour walking and running up and down the beach with Bo, playing at the shoreline, waiting for the waves as though daring them to catch them, then squealing as the water gushed over their toes. They inched their way backwards when the water came too close. Mary Kate realized she had not had so much fun in a long time.

"Having fun?" someone called.

Mary Kate turned to see Blake standing barefoot at the water's edge, watching them with a pleased expression on his face. "I put the picnic basket up there," he pointed to a picnic table. "I'm hungry—what about you two?"

"Great idea," Mary Kate looked at Hanna as they walked across to join him.

"Let's see what surprises you have tucked away in here," he said, leading the way back to the picnic bench.

Mary Kate saw that he had been considerate enough to bring down a plastic picnic cloth, napkins, paper plates and cups, a fresh pitcher of fruit punch, and bowl of water for Bo.

Mary Kate began to laugh. "You two may be in for a disappointment. After offering a picnic snack, I got home and discovered my best fare for sandwiches was peanut butter and jelly!"

"That's my favorite," Hanna said, peering into the basket.

Mary Kate pulled out the plastic-wrapped sandwiches and potato chips and a three large apples.

Hanna had sat down on the picnic bench, eagerly awaiting her food while Bo happily sunned himself in the warm sand. Blake swung his long legs over the bench and sat down, his interested gaze flicking over their snack. "Well, Hanna, I bet you think this is the perfect picnic."

"Mmmm," she said, already digging into a sandwich. "I like it better than Sue's fancy old casseroles."

"Come on, now. Sue's a good cook," Blake defended.

Hanna took control of the conversation, relating things from school and projects that had been assigned. Mary Kate was relieved to see that she was opening up to her more, talking freely about her life.

Then when the three of them had finished, Blake stood up, stretching his long legs. "Want to take a walk?"

Hanna darted over and grabbed his hand. "Dad, can we walk down to the pier?"

He glanced eastward to a long pier that looked to be half a mile in the distance.

"Think you're both up to it?" He looked from Hanna to Mary Kate.

"I'm game," she answered.

"So am I! Come on, Bo!" Hanna's blue eyes twinkled merrily, and it warmed Mary Kate's heart to see the change that had come over the little girl since the first time she had seen her.

With Hanna in the center, holding each of their hands, they began to walk toward the pier, Bo running ahead and back again. As they walked Blake talked about the development in this area of the beach, the building codes, and other general topics that interested Mary Kate. Hanna, meanwhile, was more interested in stopping for an occasional seashell. Catching on, Bo sniffed out the best shells for her.

Later, after they had returned to the chalet, Hanna grabbed her sand bucket from the porch and sat down in the sand. The day's frolic had tired her out and now she was content to sit and play while the exhausted black cocker spaniel napped beside her.

Blake brought beach chairs onto the deck and he and Mary Kate sat talking while Hanna built a sand castle.

"She's an adorable child," Mary Kate said, watching her.

"Thanks," he sighed. "And I must tell you, she thinks you're about the greatest person she's ever met. I hope you won't take offense if I suggest that she may be trying to play Cupid."

Surprise widened her brown eyes before realization dawned. She looked at Hanna then at the ocean, slightly embarrassed.

"I'm not offended," she said quietly, "but. . ." her voice

trailed. She had no idea how to express what she was thinking.

"But what?" he asked, studying her thoughtfully.

"I have the impression there is no room in your life for another woman." She turned to face him squarely.

"There hasn't been—before," he replied slowly. "I've been too preoccupied with my own personal problems."

Mary Kate nodded, understanding what he was saying.

"Still, I've missed not having a life, and I haven't had a normal one in what seems like a very long time."

"It's been rough for you, hasn't it?" Mary Kate asked sympathetically.

He nodded. "Still, I've pushed myself too hard for too long. You see," he glanced at her briefly, "I've been driven for years to succeed in my work. I suppose I've allowed it to dominate my life for too many years. It became a matter of pride to see how successful I could become, how much money I could make." He sighed, looking far out into the ocean. "Then when Charlotte became so ill, all the money and success couldn't solve the problem. The money helped of course—for a while." He said nothing more, as though he were deep in thought.

"I've been caught up in my work too. I know the feeling."

He turned to look at her curiously. "You're a very pretty girl, and you're intelligent and fun. Surely you could have married if you had wanted to."

She shrugged. "Guess I just never met the right guy."

"Not that you haven't had offers," he said, testing her.

She smiled. "My parents are very happy together, and I've looked for the same kind of commitment."

The next words came from her heart, an admission of her own philosophy, and she spoke without even thinking how he might react. "They always taught me to pray for the right man, and I have. So I can't take all the credit for not making a blunder. I've relied on God for guidance in making the right choices."

"I see," he said quietly, looking out across the ocean. "You're very religious, aren't you?"

"Religious? Funny, I don't think of myself that way, just a Christian who tries to do the right thing—most of the time," she added with a grin. "But I do see God's hand in things. For example," she hesitated, glancing at the late afternoon sun painting scarlet ribbons across the horizon, "whenever I see such beauty, I cannot understand how anyone could doubt the existence of God."

"Belief is one thing. Living up to His expectation is more difficult, I think."

"His or yours? I have a feeling you set awfully high standards for yourself, Blake Taylor. No one is perfect."

He stared into her eyes for a moment, saying nothing. Then he took a deep breath and smiled down at her. "I like being with you. I think you're very good for me."

"Blake," she began uncertainly. She wanted to talk with him about Hanna's desire to become a Christian, but she didn't want to seem like she was intruding in their lives. She was wondering how to word it.

"What is it? What did you want to say?" he prompted.

"Well," she took a deep breath, "this morning after we left church Hanna was asking me about becoming a Christian. Your mother had already talked with her about it," she added quickly. "I think she was touched by the sermon. I wanted her to talk with you. And I don't want you to think that I'm interfering," she added, watching his face carefully for a reaction.

"I don't think you're interfering at all," he said quietly. "I think you're helping—" he broke off just as Hanna came up the steps.

"That was a great sand castle you made," Mary Kate said.

"Thanks. Want to look at my seashells with me?"

"Sure." Mary Kate stood up, letting Hanna lead the way back inside.

ta

Later, Blake grilled hamburgers for them and they ate heartily, their appetites boosted by the sea breeze and the activities of the day. When finally they drove home that evening, Mary Kate felt as though she had been with them for longer than an afternoon. They had discussed many things about their lives and their plans for the future. Blake had even told her of a shopping center he planned to build five miles from their beach house. It had been a wonderful day for Mary Kate and she felt a stab of disappointment as he pulled into her driveway and she knew the day had come to an end.

Hanna was stretched out in the backseat, sound asleep with Bo curled up beside her, as Blake stopped the car and started to open his door.

"You don't need to see me to my door," she said, smiling across at him. She picked her purse up from the floorboard, glanced back at Hanna and Bo one last time, then looked quickly in his direction. "I, that is we, had a wonderful time. Thank you."

"Thank you for going," he said. He smiled at her, but there was something more in his eyes. Mary Kate didn't want to think about what that was, or what he was thinking, or what she was feeling.

Hopping out of the car, she let Bo out of the backseat

without disturbing Hanna, and they hurried up to her front door. Blake waited, his car lights illuminating her path until she had unlocked the door and turned on the inside light. Then she waved again to him and closed the door.

She leaned against the door and sighed. Her heart was soaring with joy, and she knew her plan not to get involved had backfired. She was already involved, and she didn't even care. She had never been so happy.

eight

Throughout the next two days, despite her efforts to concentrate, Mary Kate's thoughts kept drifting toward Blake, her desire to be with him increasing. She was aware of her coworkers regarding her with puzzled expressions, yet everyone remained tactfully silent.

Everyone, that is, except Coty.

"Guess who I just happened to see over on the pier on Sunday afternoon?"

Mary Kate stared at him for a moment, then remembered that he spent his weekends fishing and that he had a trailer over at the beach.

"Us?" she whispered, grinning.

"Yes, us," he whispered back, teasing her. "You're grinning like a Cheshire cat every time I see you, and there's a look in those big brown eyes that definitely has not been there before!"

Mary Kate looked up from her work, smiling dreamily.

Coty was shaking his head, looking worried. "I hate to see you get stepped on your first time out, Kid. It *is* the first time, isn't it?"

"He is a very nice man," she snapped, then glanced around to see if anyone was listening. No one was. She lowered her voice. "Your problem, Coty, is that you have no faith in human nature. In fact, you have no *faith*, period. And that's a problem," she added gently.

Coty sighed. "You have a way of setting me straight like

no one else. Except maybe Sharon." His big jaw dropped, pain settling over his face like a tragic mask.

"Coty, why don't you two get back together?" Mary Kate looked into his eyes, sensing his pain. "I know you still love her—and she loves you. I was talking to her last week when she came by to leave some mail for you. She still loves you, Coty."

"I'm so lonely without her and the children," he said, leaning against her desk and looking absolutely desolate. "But I just can't believe she'd ever forgive me for the mess I made of our marriage. Once you start lying and deceiving the way I have, Mary Kate. . ." He shook his head. "I don't guess we can work it out now."

Mary Kate stared at him for a moment. Then she reached into her shoulder bag. Plunging into its depths, she pulled out the worn New Testament that Coty had made fun of recently. "Read this, Coty," she insisted. "The answers to all your problems are in that book."

He hesitated, glancing nervously around the newsroom.

"Take it," she pushed it into his hand, breathing a sigh of relief when he accepted it awkwardly, then turned and bounded out of the newsroom.

Later, that afternoon, she was just clearing off her desk when Carey announced there was a phone call for her. A special twinkle in Carey's eye told her it might be an interesting call, and she noticed that Carey lingered for another second as she answered.

"This is Mary Kate," she said, giving Carey the eye. Laughing, Carey took her hint and strolled off.

"Hi, this is Blake. I know I'm calling you on the spur of the moment, and I apologize, but for the first time Hanna has accepted an invitation to go home with a friend for pizza, and I was wondering—"

"Yes?"

"I told Sue to go on and take the night off. That there was no point in her cooking. Could I interest you in joining me someplace for dinner?"

Mary Kate had no plans for the evening, and this time she didn't want to say no.

"As a matter of fact, you could. I'm just leaving work in about ten minutes."

"So am I. Want to meet somewhere?"

"Sure."

"How about a steak?"

Mary Kate rarely splurged that much and the choice appealed to her. "Sounds great. Where?"

He suggested a nice restaurant conveniently located. "So why don't I meet you there in, say, twenty minutes? Will that give you enough time?"

"That'll be fine," she said, opening the bottom drawer for her shoulder bag.

After she hung up, she made a dash to the ladies room to freshen up. She had chosen a polka dot dress today, pale blue with white dots, a scoop neck and cap sleeves. Her on-the-street interview had been with a young couple who were heading up a charity drive for the summer. She thought a fun type of dress would be appropriate and now she was glad she had chosen it.

Diving into her bag, she retrieved her pink-and-white striped makeup kit and unzipped it. She touched up her mascara, added a bit of blusher and lip gloss, then replaced the makeup kit, and pulled her hairbrush from the bottom of the bag. Once she had brushed the shine back in her hair, she was satisfied that she passed inspection for a dinner date. Smoothing the wrinkles from her dress, she rushed out of the ladies room and almost collided with Carey.

"Hmm. Does he look as good as he sounds?" Carey teased.

"Absolutely," Mary Kate gave her an impish grin then rushed on.

෴

Blake was waiting for her just inside the door of the restaurant still wearing a dark business suit and crisp white shirt. Mary Kate wondered how he managed to stay so neat after a long day. His hair was combed neatly in place, and the blue eyes were shining as though he enjoyed seeing her again.

"Hi." She smiled at him.

"Hi. I already have us a table."

A hostess led the way back through the crowded restaurant to a quiet table in the corner where Blake pulled out a chair for her. Once she was seated, she leaned back in the chair and inhaled the wonderful aromas that floated around her.

"Something to drink first?" an attentive server asked, laying menus before them.

"Iced tea, please," she answered.

"Coffee for me," Blake said, then looked back at Mary Kate. "It's been a long day and I need the caffeine."

"Sounds as though you were really busy."

He nodded. "It was one of those days. What about you?"

She smiled. "It was one of those days for me, as well, so maybe we need to think of better things. Like Hanna. I'm glad she's having dinner with a friend."

Blake suddenly looked more serious. "So am I. She's been something of a loner for a while now."

Mary Kate folded her hands in her lap, remembering her

conversation with Hanna about friends. "She said as much to me. Why is that, may I ask?"

He was silent for a minute, staring at the white linen tablecloth. "I guess," he looked up at her, "it began with her mother's illness. We were unable to have company because Charlotte was so sick. And then after she lost her mother, she seemed to withdraw from the other children. It was as though she didn't want to be reminded that other little girls had normal lives and she didn't. And too," he sighed, "I'm afraid I gave in to her too much during those last months. It was hard for me to discipline her, even though I realized she was cranky and difficult, at times. To be perfectly honest, she probably wasn't very pleasant to be around, and I imagine the kids avoided her as well."

The drinks were placed before them, giving Mary Kate an opportunity to frame a reply. "Well, she seemed to enjoy Sunday school, and there was no problem with her getting along with the other children."

He nodded. "I sensed that. Again, I'm grateful for your help."

She shook her head. "I only took her there. She was the one who interacted, but I will admit that her class is wonderful. I often substitute for Lisa, the teacher. She's a very sensitive, caring person, and she encourages those in her class to treat each other in the same manner. I'm sure they made Hanna feel welcome."

"Ready to order?" A handsome young server stood at their table, ready to explain the specialties of the house. He looked young and eager, and kept glancing at Mary Kate as though he recognized her. That was happening more often now, people referring to her as that "TV girl who does the on-the-street thing." She always had to laugh at that expression, but it really didn't bother her.

They both decided on steak, salad, and potatoes.

"I'll have the large T-bone, medium rare, with steak fries," Blake said.

Mary Kate winced. "I'll have the filet, but cook mine longer, please, and I'll have the baked potato."

They both chose the same kind of salad dressing. "At least we agree on that," Mary Kate laughed.

Smiling at them, the server swept up their menus and dashed off.

"Have you done anything interesting this week?" she asked conversationally.

"As a matter of fact, I had a great day today. My architect and I left at six this morning and flew up to Highlands, North Carolina, to study an interesting new building there. We got back shortly before I phoned you."

"Highlands! That's a neat place, isn't it? Very small and cozy, but popular with the upper class."

"It's become popular with everyone. It's one of my favorite vacation spots—summer as well as winter. There's skiing nearby, and I like to ski in winter, but in the summer it's really heaven. Nice and cool. The merchants have provided lots of interesting things to attract people year-round. I wanted to study the way they've developed one particular area to get some ideas for my beach development."

Mary Kate nodded. "Very smart of you."

A basket of rolls had been placed on the table and Mary Kate dived in. Her simple ham and cheese sandwich for lunch seemed hours away. She buttered a bite of roll and popped it in her mouth, then hesitated. Blake was studying her with a little grin, and she couldn't resist asking him what he was thinking.

"I enjoy watching you enjoy yourself," he said, reaching for a roll.

She licked her lips. "Try one of those," she indicated the rolls, "and you'll soon be enjoying yourself."

"I already am. I really like being with you. You're very good for me, do you know that?"

She shifted in the chair, suddenly feeling a bit uncomfortable. "Why do you say that?" she asked, concentrating on her roll.

He hesitated for a moment, as though choosing his words. "You help me relax again, to see that life is still fun."

"Of course it is," she said gently, thinking he must have suffered terribly over his wife. "Maybe you need to relax more than you do. Maybe you work too hard."

He sighed. "I do. Work has been an escape for me, I'm afraid. Since the incident with Hanna, my eyes have been opened. I'm trying to do better." His eyes met hers. "You're helping me as much as you're helping Hanna, but you probably don't realize that."

She stared at him for a moment. "No, I didn't realize that," she answered.

Their eyes had locked and now there was a new kind of tension between them, but strangely it felt good. She liked being with him, and she was glad she had taken the time to get to know him better.

Their food arrived then, diverting their thoughts, and the rest of the meal passed with general conversation about the city and some of its residents. They decided to split a piece of brownie pie, giggling like teenagers when they were handed two forks and a huge bowl overflowing with brownie, fudge sauce, and ice cream.

"I may not be able to get out of the chair," she laughed, looking across at Blake. Then suddenly something pulled her eyes toward a far corner of the restaurant where Brad and his wife Jane were taking a seat. Brad had already spotted her and his mouth was hanging open.

She quickly looked back at the dessert, but suddenly it didn't taste quite as good. Now all she wanted was to get out of the restaurant, away from Brad's prying eyes.

"I think I've had it," she said, pushing back from the table and folding her napkin over her plate.

"So have I." He motioned for the server. "Are you in a hurry to get home?"

She glanced at her watch. It was eight-thirty. "Do you realize we've been sitting here for two and a half hours?" she asked, amazed.

He chuckled. "No, but I've enjoyed every minute of it. Hanna has to be home by nine so I guess that answers my question about getting home."

She nodded as they got up from the table and left the restaurant. And she never again glanced in Brad's direction.

❧

"Brad wants to see you in his office right away," Carey informed Mary Kate as soon as she entered the bustling offices of WJAK the next morning.

Mary Kate suppressed a sigh as she stopped at her desk long enough to collect her telephone messages and place her shoulder bag in the bottom drawer.

"Good morning," she called cheerfully as she entered Brad's office.

His eyes darted up from his cluttered desk, and immediately she read the concern on his face.

"Close the door," he said, staring at her a bit differently.

Please let this be about a news story, she silently prayed, although she had a feeling she knew what was coming. He had not looked pleased about seeing her out with Blake. She closed the door and settled into the chair opposite his desk. "What's up?" she tried to sound casual as she laced her fingers in the lap of her pants suit.

"What were you doing out with Blake Taylor?" he asked in a low voice.

Her mouth fell open. "Brad, I have a right to a life after I leave here. We met for dinner, that was all." She frowned at him. "I wouldn't think my private life should interest you, anyway."

"If you were with Blake Taylor, it interests me," his eyes shot over her head to the glass wall that enclosed his office.

Automatically, she looked over her shoulder to see if someone was there, but nobody was. Then she realized this must be a highly confidential conversation they were supposed to be having.

"Why are we having this conversation, Brad?" she glared at him.

"You can't do that, Mary Kate," he said, his eyes boring through her.

"Do what?" She was thoroughly confused.

"You can't see Blake Taylor socially. Don't you realize there's still a lot of public sentiment where he's concerned? A lot of people were not convinced by the defense that he was entirely innocent."

"And you?" she asked coolly.

"I think his money got him off."

She gasped and stared at him. "That's a cruel thing to say. And very unfair. Brad, he is one of the nicest men I've ever met. He's genuinely nice, and he's devoted to his little girl,

Hanna. They've had a rotten time the past year. First, the mother's death and then—"

"I'm well aware of the conditions surrounding his family. If I'm not mistaken, I'm the one who filled you in on those circumstances."

She heaved a sigh and leaned her head against the chair. He was right, he had. She was suddenly at a loss for words. How could she respond to her boss, when in the beginning she had felt the same way he did?

"I think he was misjudged, Brad. I believe he was innocent."

Brad dropped his eyes to his desk, fumbled with a piece of paper for a moment, as though gathering his thoughts. Then he leaned back in the chair and studied her thoughtfully.

"Look, I know he's an attractive man. He has money and he's charming and—"

"Hold it," she put up her hand. "His daughter called me when she ran away, remember? Then I was invited to their house so that he could thank me for helping to locate her. I ended up taking her to Sea World, and then to Sunday school on Sunday."

She paused, wondering how best to explain how she had become drawn into the family so quickly. She looked Brad squarely in the eye and spoke to him as she would her own brother.

"Brad, I don't see the harm of going out with him. After all, he is still a prominent man in this town with lots of friends who believe he was innocent of that theft charge."

He propped his hands on the toppled stacks of work and leaned toward her. "The harm of it is that I don't want you to get hurt. I care about you. Last night the expression on your face was the perfect picture of a young woman falling in love." He paused, clearing his throat as she stared at him, wide-eyed. "Blake Taylor is a very attractive man. I can see why it would be hard for you to resist his advances."

"He has made no advances," she snapped. "And Brad, I am not going to let WJAK dictate how I spend the few leisure hours I have left after giving most of my life to this job. You have no right to do that!"

He sighed. "I understand where you're coming from, Mary Kate." He was speaking in a different tone of voice, a controlled tone that she had heard him use when he was trying to hold onto his logic before he lost his temper. "But I have to warn you. While this man is still such a controversial figure, you could be putting your job in jeopardy if you were to allow this friendship to continue."

Mary Kate stood up and stared down at him, unable to believe her ears. How could he say that? How could one's boss make such an unfair call?

"I'm not sure you have the right to make that kind of threat, Brad." She was fighting her temper now, and she knew she had to get out of his office before she said something she would regret. She turned to go.

"Wait," Brad stood up, staring across the desk at her. "I'm not making any threats, Mary Kate. And I will try to respect your privacy. I'm just asking you to wait a while. Is that fair enough?"

She hesitated, her hand on the knob. She wanted to turn and yell NO, but her common sense was slowly returning, and in her mind's eye she recalled her attempts to balance her checkbook each month. She had foolishly overspent after moving here, and now she was trying to get her bills paid off. Furthermore, she liked her job; it had been very important to her, and it still was. More than Blake Taylor, she told herself.

She bobbed her dark head slowly and glanced back over her shoulder. "Okay," she said and walked out of the office.

As usual, she became caught up in her work, trying to meet all the demands of her hectic job. She tried not to think of Blake and Hanna when she went home feeling lonely every day, but by Thursday evening, Blake broke the silence.

The phone rang after she had curled up on the sofa with a book and when she answered, she heard his smooth rich voice.

"Are you having a good week?" he asked, his tone friendly and polite.

She rolled her eyes, thinking he had no way of knowing the veiled threat Brad had tossed at her first thing Wednesday morning. "A typically busy one," she answered. "And you?"

"Typically busy too," he said. "Hanna is already talking about Sunday school again, and I was wondering if I could entice you for Sunday lunch and another trip to our beach house."

Mary Kate took a slow deep breath. What was she going to do? As a Christian, she had to lead Hanna gently along the road to becoming a Christian; but she had to do this without seeing Blake. But then she had another thought. "Could you join us for church?"

He sighed. "Mary Kate, I'm not quite ready for that. But I will be soon, if you'll just give me a little more time. For the first time in a long while, I got my Bible out and read a few passages."

Tears filled Mary Kate's eyes. How could she walk away from this man; on the other hand, how could she defy her boss?

"So could you join Hanna for Sunday school one more time?" he asked.

She nodded her head, hating the conflict that had developed. "I'll be happy to pick her up as usual. But I can't join you afterwards. I'm sorry."

"Oh." She heard the disappointment in his voice, but he quickly recovered. "I should have called sooner, but the week just got away from me and—"

"That's quite all right," she said, more brusquely than she intended. "I understand, and it wouldn't have mattered. I. . . already had plans."

Like watering the plants and reading the Sunday paper.

"Why don't I drop Hanna off at Sunday school, then? The least I can do is drive her there, if you're willing to bring her home."

Bring her home. How could she say no? "I'll be glad to do that," she answered and gave him the time to drop Hanna off. "Also," she added, "please have her come in the side door on Beckam Street. I'll be waiting there for her."

There was a momentary pause, and she sensed he was about to say more, so she rushed to fill the silence.

"So I'll see her then. And thanks for calling," she said hurriedly.

He took the hint and said good-bye. After she hung up the phone, she grabbed a throw pillow and tossed it across the floor. This was so unfair. At last she had found someone she could truly care for, a kind and decent man, and a little girl who needed her. Here was her chance to witness where it was sorely needed, and now Brad had put an end to it. She jumped up from the sofa and began to pace circles around the living room, trying to vent her frustration.

Maybe not an end, just a delay, she thought, consoling herself. If she could keep making excuses to Blake, maybe in time, she could have another talk with Brad, and things would change. Or maybe her desire to see Blake would change. But she doubted that. She sank back onto the sofa, her knees drawn to her chin.

"God, please help me with this situation. I don't know what to do," she sighed, feeling sick at heart.

She thought of the afternoon's conversation with Brad. He had called her into his office and asked her if she would like to audition for anchor of the evening news. Justin, their anchor for the past three years, was accepting a job in Chicago and would be leaving soon. The station's general manager had set aside a couple of hours tomorrow to audition prospects for the job.

"This is a good opportunity for you, Mary Kate," Brad had said with a beaming smile.

Looking at him, she couldn't resist the sneaking suspicion that he was merely trying to make amends for telling her she shouldn't see Blake Taylor. Still, she knew she was fortunate to be offered this opportunity. At one time, it had been her driving ambition, and now she was anxious to see if the job still appealed to her. On the other hand, if that job became available, she would miss her daily contact with people on a personal basis. She had tried to bring some compassion to the world of hard news, inject some kindness and sympathy for those who needed it.

She stretched out on the sofa and reminded herself she had to get a good night's sleep so she would look her best for tomorrow. She couldn't let personal problems get in the way now—not when she had an opportunity for a real career advancement.

Closing her eyes, she tried to rationalize the situation. She would take Hanna to Sunday school, thus keeping her promise to Hanna, and maybe even to God, and she would try out for the anchor job just to please Brad—and maybe herself.

&

"With bone structure like yours, today's job is a snap!" smiled Annie, the makeup artist, as she whisked rose blusher onto Mary Kate's smooth, beige skin.

"You're just talented," Mary Kate countered, studying her face in the mirror. Outlined in smoky eye shadow, her brown eyes appeared deeper, more mysterious, while her dark hair, swept back from her face in a sophisticated twist, revealed more prominently her classic features. The look didn't feel quite right, but she kept silent, choosing to trust the opinion of the experts.

Her eyes inched downward to the sophisticated navy linen suit. The straight, tailored look was offset by the bright red bow of a red silk blouse. Somehow the outfit managed to achieve just the right touch of sophistication without being too formal. The wardrobe consultant had suggested the suit, on loan from one of the top stores, as opposed to Mary Kate's preference for loose, flowing dresses.

"You need to look older," the wardrobe lady had stated tactfully.

"Why do I want to look *older?*" Mary Kate had stared at her wide-eyed.

"Because it's difficult to believe you're a day over twenty-one now. This type of job requires a bit of sophistication."

"Then maybe it isn't right for me," Mary Kate sighed, then grinned at the woman. "I'm really a simple gal at heart."

She said as much to the makeup artist now, emphasizing that she didn't want to stray too far from the person she really was. "And I don't think the people of Seabreeze want me to come across drastically changed. It'll ruin my image," she teased and they both laughed.

"Well, heaven forbid that we ruin your image. What if we just dress it up a bit?"

Mary Kate bobbed her sleek dark hair in an emphatic nod. "I guess that's okay."

The possibility of getting made-up to go before a television camera each evening, looking far too glamorous and sophisticated for her own taste, made her question her interest in being an anchor.

"I don't know why I let myself get talked into this," she mumbled, leaning back in the chair with a regretful sigh. "There are other people more qualified."

"I hear you're the favorite," Annie whispered. "Besides, you mustn't resist opportunity when it knocks!" She winked at Mary Kate as she reached for a can of hair spray and enveloped her in a cloud of mist.

"Mary Kate? You're on next." A technician popped his head around the door. "Come on into the control room."

"Thanks, Annie," Mary Kate said, taking a deep breath as she cast one last glance in the mirror. "You've worked your magic."

"You make my work easy," Annie laughed, tapping her on the shoulder. "Good luck, Mary Kate."

"Thanks again." She hurried out the door and down the long corridor leading to the stairway.

As she climbed the narrow flight of stairs, her heart began to hammer, not in fear, but in response to the step she was taking. *Is this really what I want? To be a television anchor?* The question brought a tiny frown to settle between her brown brows as she opened the door and slipped quietly into the control room.

Squinting against the dimness as the technicians adjusted

controls, she peered through the glass window to the stage below where a highly-respected anchor from a Jacksonville station sat reading a script to Mr. Lucas, the general manager, seated in the front row.

"You're next," someone whispered, and she nodded in reply, hurrying out the door and down the back steps to the stage.

Mary Kate stood in the background analyzing the smooth delivery of the man as he finished his last line and glanced expectantly toward the front row. He was answered with a brisk nod before Mary Kate was waved onto the stage.

She squared her shoulders and walked quickly to the small rectangular platform that served as the news desk. Seating herself, she scanned the two typewritten sheets as she cleared her throat.

"You know what to do," one technician whispered, as he clipped the tiny microphone to her collar. "Just flash that all-American smile."

Given the nod, she began to read, her voice ringing across the quiet stage as she directed her attention to Camera One, only vaguely aware of Mr. Lucas, leaning forward in the front row. After she had finished, she blinked into the bright lights, waiting for a response. When there was none, she stood to leave.

"Ms. Moore?"

She paused, turning back.

"Well done." The silver-haired Thomas Lucas strolled up to her, his hand extended.

"Thank you," she nodded, gripping his hand.

"And may I say you do a splendid job with your on-the-street interviews? I assume you're aware of the ratings."

"Yes," she replied modestly, taking in the distinguished

man who controlled the firing and hiring of employees with a mere nod of his silver head.

"You don't sound as southern as we had expected. Normally, we're sensitive about accents, but the public seems to be quite taken with yours. In fact, you've brought a bit of a new dimension to television newscasting."

She shifted uncomfortably, wondering how to reply. She quickly decided to center the conversation on Justin, making a complimentary remark about his popularity as news anchor. Soon, a secretary was waving a telephone toward the older man, and she breathed a deep sigh of relief when he nodded and went to accept the phone call.

Mary Kate returned to her desk, filled with an uneasiness she couldn't define. She had been staring blankly at a stack of telephone messages when Carey tapped her on the shoulder and pointed to her ringing telephone. She dived for it, self-consciously aware that she was the object of a few questioning stares.

As soon as she spoke a quick hello, Hanna's eager little voice filled her ears, bringing a smile of pleasure to her face.

"Hanna, I'm glad to hear from you!" she exclaimed, cradling the phone against her shoulder while she flipped idly through the telephone messages.

"Are we still going to Sunday school this Sunday?"

"Of course. Didn't your dad tell you I was expecting you?"

"Yes. I just wanted to know if you could stay for lunch."

She was about to offer a quick refusal when Hanna spoke again, changing the direction of her thoughts.

"Dad's been called someplace for a meeting Sunday. He's leaving town as soon as he drops me off at Sunday school if you can still bring me home. Sue will be here. She'll fix our lunch."

Mary Kate hesitated. If Blake was not going to be at home,

why not have lunch with Hanna? She would enjoy being with her, and she hated the thought of the little girl eating alone. Well, Sue would be there, but still. . .

"Okay, tell you what. I'll stay for lunch and visit a while. Then I'll have to run."

"I'll see you Sunday," Hanna said, obviously excited about the prospect.

"Right. See you then. Thanks for calling," she added before she hung up.

It occurred to her that Blake might find it odd that she could suddenly change her plans and have lunch, knowing he was going out of town. She sighed. It couldn't be helped. She couldn't please everyone.

She returned to the phone messages that awaited her, trying again to concentrate on her job.

&.

The announcement became official by the end of the day. Mary Kate Moore was the new co-anchor of WJAK evening news. The promotion was received with mixed reactions— surprise and pleasure among her friends, envy and doubt among a few of her coworkers. Brad had been sincere in his congratulations, but she sensed a wariness in Coty, with whom she had worked closely for the past year as her number one cameraman. He seemed to be able to read her mind when others could not.

Mary Kate was not quite sure how she felt. There was no question that she was excited and pleased, in one sense. But somewhere deep in her soul, there was a restlessness, an unease she could not quite define.

Late that afternoon, as she was winding up her work at the desk, her telephone rang. Wearily, she answered it then snapped to attention at the sound of Blake's voice.

nine

"I just heard the news," he said. "Congratulations."

"Oh," she plunged a hand through her hair and automatically glanced at Brad's office. The lights were out. He had already gone home for the evening. "Thanks. I think."

"You think?" he laughed. "I'm sure you'll be great. This calls for a celebration. How about dinner?"

The truth was, she would have adored going out to a restaurant and having a nice meal with Blake. She was starving. But then she remembered Brad's warning and she heaved a sigh. "I'm afraid the day has drained me completely. All I want to do is go home and put my feet up on the coffee table."

"That's even better."

She hiked an eyebrow. "I beg your pardon?"

"I'm calling from my car phone, and as we speak I'm turning into the grocery. I'll pick up a few things. I'm in a cooking mood, so just indulge me. You see, you can still go home and put your feet up on the coffee table. And your dinner will be waiting for you. Have I tempted you sufficiently?"

Mary Kate's heart was racing. *How can I get out of this? And why do I even want to?* she thought crossly, as she glared at Brad's empty office.

"Well, the problem is," she said, looking wildly around the newsroom, "I can't even leave this place for another thirty minutes. I'm waiting on a phone call and—"

"That'll be perfect. I'll have dinner ready when you walk

through the door. Where do you hide the key?"

"The key?" she echoed, feeling as though every defense she put up was being shot down with lightning speed.

"Every woman keeps an extra key hidden somewhere near her door," he continued pleasantly, "unless you are one of those rare sorts who never locks yourself out."

She couldn't resist laughing at that. He was so right. She did have a key hidden in the flowerpot. And what Brad didn't know wouldn't hurt him. Or her. There was no chance of her running into anyone if they were at her apartment. Furthermore, she had earned a little celebration and she hated the thought of celebrating alone.

"Okay. Look in the flowerpot. On the back side, you'll find a spare key tucked under a long leaf."

He groaned. "That's way too easy. I'll find a better hiding place for you. See you when you get there." With that he hung up, giving her no more time to refuse. He had probably planned it that way, she decided with a wry grin.

Trying not to remember the state of her duplex, she cleared off her desk and returned a couple of phone calls. By the time she freshened up in the ladies lounge and locked up for the night, she had managed to use up the thirty minutes she claimed as an excuse earlier—the excuse that got her nowhere with Blake.

She smiled to herself as she hurried to her car. It was a summer evening and still daylight. The air felt warm and balmy against her cheeks, and she quickened her steps, looking forward to the evening ahead. She realized that she liked a take-charge man like Blake. He wasn't pushy, yet he wasn't the wimp that Frank Haroldson had been, whom she had dated briefly last year then given up on him when she was forced to make all the decisions about where they ate or what

movie they saw. Sometimes, after work, it seemed her brain
had shut down and refused to function. This was one of those
times, and it was actually a relief to have someone else calling the shots.

❧

"Surprise!"

Blake greeted her at her door, dressed in jeans and a blue
button-down shirt, a dish towel knotted thickly about his
waist.

"I like your apron," Mary Kate burst into laughter as she
hurried inside and closed the door. She had already taken
note of the fact that his black car was conspicuously parked
in her driveway, but soon it would be dark and she was
blessed with neighbors who minded their own business.

The weariness that seemed to be dragging at her heels all
day suddenly disappeared, replaced by a warm glow tingling through her veins.

"Do come in," he stepped aside, waving dramatically with
his arm. "I've timed the meal just right. Are you impressed?"

"Definitely. What is that heavenly smell?" She sniffed the
spicy aromas as she followed him to the kitchen.

"Lasagna."

"Mmm," she sighed, glancing around. To her relief, the
place was fairly neat and Bo was behaving himself, as well.
She couldn't decide if her little dog was intimidated or fas-
cinated by Blake.

"How did Bo react to you coming in alone?" she asked
curiously.

"Suspiciously at first. Then I gave him a tiny sample of
dinner and we've been best friends ever since."

She laughed again, suddenly feeling wonderful. It was so
unfair for Brad to deny her an innocent good time. And how

could anyone suspect that this dear man could ever be a thief? It was ridiculous!

"I've been slaving away for hours," he sighed, but he was obviously teasing. He peered into the oven then closed the door and turned back to her. "I hope you're impressed."

Her eyes widened as she took in his neatly combed hair and deep blue eyes. "I am," she replied, wondering if she was referring to the meal or the man.

"Used to be one of my specialties," he said, taking her handbag from her and placing it on a chair. Then he led her toward the living room sofa. "Now kick off those weapons and put your aching feet on the coffee table as you had planned to do."

She sighed, pleased to be doing as she was told. "Shouldn't I set the table or something?" she asked, feeling guilty.

"You should do nothing other than look pretty, which seems to be easy for you."

Mary Kate sank onto the sofa and kicked off her high heels. He towered over her, as though waiting for her to obey. Once her stocking feet were placed squarely on the coffee table, he leaned down and picked up a slim foot.

"What do you think you're doing?" she asked in surprise.

"I'm rubbing your tired feet," he said matter-of-factly as her stiff muscles began to relax when he gently messaged her feet.

She took a deep breath and sighed with relief as the aching disappeared beneath his skilled fingers.

"Why do women wear those uncomfortable things?" he asked, frowning at her three-inch navy spikes.

"Normally, I don't. But this morning we had a meeting with the mayor and his staff, and I was trying to look professional."

His eyes ran down her white linen dress with its contrasting navy belt and buttons and he nodded approvingly. "You look very professional. Want to change into something comfortable?"

"I think I'd prefer having my feet rubbed and then watching you prepare my dinner," she said sleepily.

"I wouldn't mind that." The serious blue gaze held her captive for several seconds. The electrical awareness that had surrounded their relationship mounted as they looked at one another. Suddenly, Mary Kate took a breath and forced her attention to the clock on the mantle.

"I think I would like to slip into a pair of jeans."

Just then the oven timer buzzed and Blake leapt to his feet. "Perfect timing," he said, hurrying back to the kitchen.

While he rattled around in the kitchen, Mary Kate hurried to her bedroom and closed the door. For one insane moment, she almost felt an impulse to turn the key in the lock. *What am I doing with this man, letting him rub my feet, cook my dinner, come to my home? Brad asked me to avoid him, and now I seem to be rushing headlong into his arms.*

She hurried to the closet door, yanking down the padded hanger for her dress. She unbuttoned the dress and skimmed out of it, then opened the bureau drawer and reached for her baggy jeans and old loafers. *Definitely unsexy,* she decided with approval. To further her image she opened another drawer and retrieved the most unfeminine T-shirt she owned. A huge black shirt that begged everyone to save the baby whales. And it hung from her small body as though she, too, were a baby whale. *Good, maybe he will lose interest,* she thought, although she dared not ask her heart if that was what she really wanted.

She caught sight of her reflection in the dresser mirror and chose not to put on more lip gloss or dab a powdered brush over her face to alter the shine. Her only concession to good grooming was to grab the hairbrush and swing it through her dark hair, so that it waved neatly about her face. And she did that *for myself,* she argued silently.

She returned to the kitchen, her expression serious, as she assessed the table and realized that there was something she could do after all.

She padded barefoot across to the china cabinet. Opening the louvered doors, she pulled out her best dinner plates, along with her crystal water goblets and gleaming silverware. First she laid out the place mats, then she set the table. She glanced over her shoulder. "Are we drinking water?" she asked, matter-of-factly.

He hiked an eyebrow, as though sensing her change in mood. "Yes, madam, we are. Unless you'd like me to sprint out for champagne."

"I don't drink."

"Good girl. How about a glass of milk?"

She burst into laughter, unable to control herself. She was beginning to remind herself of Frank Haroldson who usually went to sleep in the movies she recommended. "I did make some fresh tea last night," she admitted. "Does that sound okay to you?"

"Sounds perfect."

She sniffed appreciatively as she passed the stove on her way to the refrigerator. "When did you learn to cook?" she asked, pulling out the pitcher of tea and reaching into the refrigerator for a tiny bowl of sliced lemon.

"During my summers between college. My uncle owned a nice restaurant in Chattanooga and kept me in work and dollars. I quit cooking for a while," he called from the kitchen as she returned to the dining room table to pour tea. "Then I married a woman who couldn't cook, and I found myself rattling the pots and pans again. I did the cooking during the first years of marriage. Then, as I became more prosperous, I hired a cook who, incidentally, was not nearly as good as Sue. When we moved here, we found a real treasure in her."

"She's a very nice lady," Mary Kate agreed, as she went back to the kitchen for the dish of lemons and her special crystal salt and pepper shakers. She stood assessing the dining room table a moment, wondering if she had missed anything.

Blake came forward, proudly bearing his lasagna in her best casserole dish. Returning to the kitchen, he opened the oven door and pulled out a pan of rolls.

"Compliments of the nearest bakery," he said, as she handed him a bread basket.

"I like your honesty," she teased. "I might have been tempted to claim them as some I had spent half the afternoon kneading and coddling."

He shook his head as he swept past her with the rolls. "Nope, you're too honest."

As he removed the towel from his waist, he began to frown. "I forgot to pick up a salad."

"No problem." She walked to the refrigerator and pulled out a jar of applesauce. "Will this substitute?"

"Perfect," he nodded, as she spooned a generous amount into a small serving bowl and took it to the table.

He turned and pulled her chair back for her. She sat down and motioned him to follow. "Let's get started."

As he took his seat, she bowed her head, offering grace for the meal. When she finished, she unfolded her napkin and lifted her fork, eager to sample his food. After two bites, she sighed and looked at him. "This is delicious. You're an excellent cook."

He shrugged. "I was afraid I might have lost my touch. It's been a while since I've tied on an apron. But I do hope you enjoy the meal."

She smiled at him, feeling her defenses fly away again. "This was very thoughtful of you, Blake."

"Actually, my motive was more selfish than you think. I figured if I could bribe you with food, I could see you again. I'm beginning to realize something, though." He lowered his fork to his plate, his eyes meeting hers. "Sitting here with you tonight, enjoying a quiet meal together, makes me realize what I've been missing." He turned back to his food.

Mary Kate looked at him with a sinking heart. Of course he had no idea that she had been warned by her boss to stay away from him, at least until the controversy about the trial died down. What was she going to do? She sincerely enjoyed being with this man.

"So are you excited about your new job?" he asked, looking back at her.

Mentally, she shifted gears, considering his question. "To be perfectly honest, I'm not sure how I feel about this job." She realized she was aching for someone to talk with. She had already spoken to her parents, but she needed to talk to someone more objective.

She touched the napkin to her mouth and looked into his eyes. "Maybe I should have taken more time before accepting the offer," she admitted, "but it seemed like the sensible thing to do."

"Do I hear a note of uncertainty in your voice?" he asked.

"Maybe. But I would be crazy not to take it." She paused for a fraction of a second. "Wouldn't I?"

He stopped chewing and studied her for a moment. "Not

if it doesn't suit you." He smiled, creating a glow in his deep blue eyes. "I think you're just having a slight case of nerves. You'll be great, and I must admit you're a lot prettier than Justin!"

She laughed too, relieved to have someone pointing out the funny side of the situation. "Well, I'll see how it goes. If I despise the job, I can always quit and go back to doing my on-the-street interviews. You know, Blake, I think that's really what's bothering me. I liked the human contact I had with those people."

"You did it so well."

"Thanks. But anyway, I've taken the plunge so I might as well see it through."

She had been so grateful to talk about her new job, then again she remembered Brad's stern warning. This time it depressed her immensely. Maybe she wasn't going to let Brad Wilson be such a dictator, after all.

"Well, in any case, I think you'll do a great job. Hanna tells me she called you earlier about Sunday. Now that you're aware I have to leave town, I really appreciate your taking the time to have lunch with Hanna. You already told me you had a busy afternoon."

She leaned back in the kitchen chair, her appetite gone. He was being so nice about this that she actually felt guilty. "Well, how can anyone say no to Hanna?" she asked lightly.

He laughed. "I can't, that's for sure. But I must admit, knowing that you're having lunch at my house tempts me to delay my trip to Montgomery for a couple more hours. But I really can't."

"Duty calls," she quipped, relieved that he wasn't changing his mind.

"Right. Anyway, thanks again for seeing her home and

having lunch with her."

"My pleasure," she said, realizing she truly meant it. "Have a safe trip to Montgomery." Then she thought of something else. "You really enjoy your work, don't you?"

He nodded. "Even when I was a little guy, I was always drawing buildings and funny cubicles for shopping centers. Mom and Dad encouraged me to pursue it as a career. In that respect, I've been lucky. What about you? How did you get into television broadcasting?"

"It's kind of funny, actually." Her brown eyes drifted into space, remembering. "Dad owns a small appliance store in Dothan. He sold TVs. He also had a repairman who worked on used ones. One day he brought home a set with just the screen—the insides were missing. He thought his kids could have fun "being on television." The others soon bored with the game, but not me. I would grab a cooking spoon for a mike and report the day's events. Mom was a dear; she always allowed me to interview her."

They both laughed then, and began to talk about their childhood. Mary Kate was pleased to learn that he, too, had come from a middle-class background and they actually had quite a bit in common.

They sat at the table for an hour talking, then Blake glanced at his watch. "Let's get these dishes done, then I have to shove off. I promised Sue she could leave by nine."

"Please. I'll do the dishes. I'd rather you go home and spend some time with Hanna."

He hesitated, glancing over the table.

"I'm serious," she said, coming to her feet. "Thanks for dinner."

"You're welcome."

As they stood up, looking across at one another, Mary Kate

realized something was about to happen between them. He leaned forward, tilted her chin back, and pressed his lips to hers, lightly at first. Then the kiss deepened and her heart began to hammer wildly. She had to stop this. *Now!*

She pulled back and looked into his eyes and knew, with a sinking heart, that she was falling in love with this man. *I can't. Not yet.* She had to put on the brakes somehow. Dropping her gaze, she quickly turned her attention to gathering up the dishes and rushing to the sink with them.

For a moment, she caught the flicker of surprise on his face, but he was a good sport about it. "Well, see you. . . soon, I guess."

"Yes, and tell Hanna hello for me," she called from the kitchen. She didn't even offer to see him to the door, for she knew it could lead to another kiss, and she was already more than a little rattled. She had never felt this way about a man, and now that she did, she had fallen for one she couldn't have.

"Good night," he called again as she heard the door open.

"Good night, Blake," she called back and then the door closed.

She stood at the kitchen sink, staring at the dishes. Even if Brad hadn't warned her, it only made sense to move slowly with a guy like Blake Taylor. Older. Experienced. A widower. And, too, she reminded herself, he had told her that she was the first person he had gone out with since his wife's death. She didn't want this to be one of those rebound relationships she was always hearing about.

She sank against the sink, her lips pressed tightly together, her eyes closed for a moment. She could hear his car start up in the driveway, and she only hoped she had not been rude.

She could have cared less about the dishes at that moment as she looked down at Bo, standing beside her, wagging his tail affectionately.

"You hungry?" she asked. She retrieved his round white bowl from its place beside the refrigerator and filled it with leftovers.

While Bo smacked away, she refilled her tea glass and wandered into the living room. She plopped on the sofa, took a sip of tea, and tried to remember the facts that had led Blake to be charged for jewelry theft.

The jewelry had been found at his house. He had been in the store the same day the jewelry disappeared—what else? He had an alibi for the time the pieces were actually spotted missing from their boxes, but he had looked at those same pieces. She sighed, not feeling so good. That was pretty strong evidence.

What else? There was a designer handbag Mrs. Taylor had admired, along with an expensive silk scarf that disappeared after the couple had been in an exclusive store in town. Mrs. Taylor had been very sick and in a wheelchair. All due respect had been paid to Charlotte Taylor, but that did not absolve the fact that several thousand dollars worth of merchandise was taken.

But Blake could have bought those pieces for her. *Why didn't he?*

That one fact nagged at Mary Kate more than any other. He was obviously doing well in his business, he had the money. So, if his wife liked the jewelry, the handbag, the scarf, why didn't he buy them? And how could he just steal them right from under the noses of the salespeople?

She shook her head, staring into space. It didn't make sense to her. What *had* made sense and constituted the case against him was the search warrant that had turned up the missing valuables hidden in the back of a bureau drawer. With the exception of one exquisite ruby ring. That piece of jewelry was never found, and like the others, Blake claimed to know nothing about it.

The defense hammered hard against the fact that nobody saw him take the jewelry, that someone could have set him up, then upon fear of being caught planted the jewelry. To back up this theory, there had been a break-in at the Taylor home which had set off the security system. The police had arrived to find no burglar and, conveniently, the family was away at the time, and Sue, the housekeeper, was not on duty. So nobody could prove that Taylor himself had not broken the glass pane of his French doors to set off the alarm. Countering that theory, however, was the fact that the family had gone to a Christmas play at school, even though Charlotte had gone in a wheelchair. The only item that appeared to be missing was a VCR, which indicated the burglar had not made it past the living room when he heard the sirens coming. On the other hand, the prosecution argued that Blake Taylor could have set this up as well.

His most convincing defense was the fact that he did have a solid alibi for the times the jewelry was actually stolen, and one clerk claimed to have seen the pieces after the Taylors left the store. Since there was no explanation for that, the prosecution paraded out the salesclerk's indebtedness and subtly suggested she might have taken a bribe. It was a low blow on their part, and it had failed to work. Since nobody had seen Blake Taylor take the jewelry, and there was no solid evidence against him, other than finding the pieces at his house, the jury had deliberated for an appalling amount of time and the opposition had caved in.

A verdict of not guilty had finally been reached.

As Mary Kate went over the facts, she realized there was enough suspicion still hanging over his head to sully his reputation, even though he was recognized as one of the most talented developers in the state. Still, that was his business life. Apparently, his personal life still suffered. And now she was suffering too.

Life seemed so unfair at times. Her eyes lifted toward the ceiling. "God, I just don't understand the way things go on down here." For years, she had been looking for a man with the qualities of Blake Taylor. She had met some nice guys, but there was always something lacking. Now with Blake, all the chemistry was there. *Too much chemistry,* she thought, kicking at the ottoman. If she didn't keep her distance, he was going to steal her heart. And she just couldn't let that happen. Particularly not now when she was in the limelight more than ever.

ten

The next day went smoothly and everyone was wonderful to her.

When she saw Brad she tried to forget that Blake had prepared dinner for her the evening before; instead, she concentrated on the news she would deliver during the six o'clock newscast. And yet, at three in the afternoon she felt a keen disappointment sitting at her desk, watching her replacement leave with the camera crew to cover a story on the animal shelter. It occurred to her that she might have chosen a job that was going to bore her, even though it meant a promotion in status and pay.

At the appointed time, she got up from her desk and went to Annie's office, ready to be "fixed up" for her newscast.

❧

The illuminated numbers on her bedside clock glared a ridiculous 12:10 and still sleep evaded her. It was useless to lie there and flop from one side of the bed to the other. Tossing the covers back, she dragged herself back into the kitchen and made a cup of hot chocolate. The congratulatory flowers from her parents, a flood of phone calls from fans, and today's wide smile on both Mr. Lucas's and Brad Wilson's faces should have combined to make her ecstatic. Or at least give her sweet dreams. So what had happened? Why did she feel such a void in her heart? Was it true, as she had heard, that a long awaited goal, once achieved, often left one empty and unfulfilled?

Depends on the goal, she thought dully, as she sank into a kitchen chair and sipped her hot chocolate. Bo came trudging out from his kitchen bed, sleepy and confused, to see what was going on. Halfheartedly licking her hand, he seemed to sense that she needed consolation for some reason.

"Thanks, Pal," she smiled, stroking his soft black fur. "You're a true friend. And a good listener," she added, as he tilted his head sideways, enjoyed the feeling of being rubbed behind his ears. "It's not as though I've rocketed to the status of a major network anchor, is it? This is merely the top rung of the local ladder—not New York, for heaven's sake." But it was a beginning, if she were serious about pursuing her career.

Oddly, the scene that flashed through her mind surprised her. She saw herself back at Sunday school, laughing with the children, playing games, feeling a warmth in her heart that had come no other way. She doubted that even being a talk show hostess would bring the heady glow she had always thought accompanied such a position.

At least not for her.

"Maybe at heart I'm just a homebody who likes having a cocker spaniel and a little girl like Hanna in my life. Not to mention her irresistible father! But what am I going to do?"

Tears filled her eyes as she finished her hot chocolate and rinsed her cup. This time when she returned to bed, she left the lamp on and reached for her Bible. She needed a kind of wisdom that she would find only there.

❧

On Sunday she waited for Hanna at the side door, and at exactly the appointed hour, the black sports sedan pulled to the curb and Blake got out. He came around to the passenger's side and opened the door for Hanna who hopped out, looking beautiful in a ruffled, sky-blue dress with a small blue satin ribbon in her blond hair. Blake walked her to the sidewalk then glanced up at the door where Mary Kate waved to him. He waved back then got into his car as Hanna ran up the sidewalk to meet her.

"Hi, Mary Kate!" Hanna's blue eyes were glowing.

"Hi, Hanna. You look wonderful. Here, let me do one little thing." She smoothed down a lock of hair near the crown of her head that she had obviously mussed as she sat against the seat in the car. "Ready for Sunday school?"

She nodded happily, linking her arm through Mary Kate's. They turned down the corridor and headed for the eight-year-old's classroom. A thought suddenly occurred to Mary Kate. "Want to stay for church? I could give Sue a call and tell her when we'll be home."

Hanna tilted her head and looked up at Mary Kate. "I guess so. If the preacher isn't boring."

As it turned out the preacher's sermon was about the kind of faith that had prompted Noah to build the ark, and Hanna had learned enough about the ark in Sunday school to perk her interest, so she wasn't bored. The music was good, and today's special was given by a group of college students who seemed to interest Hanna. When the altar call was given, Hanna turned and glanced seriously at Mary Kate. For a moment, Mary Kate wondered if she should ask Hanna if she wanted to walk down the aisle and give her heart to God. Then Hanna looked down at her hands, folded demurely in her lap and the moment passed.

Don't push her, Mary Kate warned herself. *When the time is right, she will know it. And I will too.*

After the church service, they drove home with Hanna talking incessantly. She seemed to be in great spirits and told Mary Kate all about her week at school. Then she turned in the seat and studied Mary Kate quietly for a moment. "Dad's been happier lately, too. But he was disappointed that you couldn't go to the beach with us this afternoon."

Mary Kate concentrated on turning into the driveway. "Well, as it turned out, he had to go to Montgomery anyway."

"How come you said you couldn't eat with us and then you changed your mind?"

Mary Kate slowed the car and cut the engine. She turned to Hanna. "To be honest, I couldn't stand the thought of you having lunch without your father. But I won't even be able to stay and help Sue with the dishes," she teased. "I'm still busy this afternoon."

It seemed a more logical answer than admitting she had tried to avoid Blake.

The answer seemed to satisfy Hanna as she reached for the door and hopped out of the car. Mary Kate joined her. Arm in arm they went up the front steps, singing a song Hanna had learned in Sunday school.

Sue met them at the door with a welcoming smile for Mary Kate. "Thanks for joining us. I understand you have a busy schedule."

"Well, not too busy to enjoy being with Hanna."

Sue looked at her curiously for a moment, as though reading what had been left unspoken. *Being with Hanna but not her father.* Then Sue turned to Hanna. "Now if you'll just run up and change clothes, I'll have everything on the table by the time you get back."

"May I do something to help?" Mary Kate offered, laying her purse on a table and following Sue to the kitchen.

"Mary Kate?" Hanna paused on the first stair and looked at Mary Kate. "Do you want to see a picture of my mother?"

Mary Kate was taken aback by the unexpected question.

Automatically, she glanced at Sue who had lowered her eyes, offering her no excuse to avoid Hanna's question.

Mary Kate cleared her throat. "Well, er, if you want me to."

"Come on upstairs," Hanna beckoned.

Feeling more than a little awkward, Mary Kate followed Hanna up the stairs and into a spacious room which Mary Kate instantly recognized as Blake's room. She froze in the doorway, feeling like an intruder.

"Come on in," Hanna looked puzzled by Mary Kate's hesitation.

Mary Kate inched her way into the room following Hanna to a large, gilt-framed portrait. Mary Kate found herself looking into the face of the striking beauty who had married Blake and given birth to Hanna. A cloud of golden brown hair framed a heart-shaped face, the complexion flawless. The features were small and perfect; the mouth reserved, lifted in only a half-smile. Yet the enormous blue eyes were captivating, tilting upwards beneath thick lashes.

There was no denying that Charlotte Taylor was one of the prettiest women Mary Kate had ever seen.

"She's very beautiful, Hanna." She glanced down at the little girl who was still staring at her mother.

She nodded. "But she didn't laugh a lot the way you do."

Puzzled by that remark, Mary Kate turned from the picture. Her eyes scanned the room, inspecting the massive furniture of a man's room, inhaling the scent of Blake's aftershave still lingering in the air.

Despite Sue's attempts at housekeeping, the room reflected a lived-in atmosphere. Books spilled over tables, a discarded jacket was flung over a chair, and dusty golf shoes sprawled in a corner. In her innocent sweep of the room, Mary Kate's eyes fell on the intimate photograph resting on the bedside table. It was a picture of Blake and Charlotte with an infant Hanna nestled between them. The couple gazed into each other's eyes as though there was no one else in all the world.

Mary Kate turned away, sick at heart, unable to distinguish whether her pain was born out of sadness for the deep love Blake had lost, or if the picture merely reaffirmed what she had already feared—that no woman could ever replace the beautiful Charlotte in Blake's heart and mind.

"I'll change clothes now," Hanna said, her voice surprisingly lighthearted. They left the room and Hanna darted down the corridor to the next bedroom. For a moment, Mary Kate stood awkwardly in the hall. "I'll help Sue," she called, feeling a bit silly, for Hanna didn't seem to care.

She turned and retraced her steps back down the stairs to the kitchen. When she entered, Sue was removing something from the oven. The heat had curled the ends of her hair around her rosy cheeks, but her eyes held an odd expression. She turned back to the casserole she was placing on the stove.

"What can I do to help?" Mary Kate asked, her fingers twitching uselessly at her side.

"Well. . .how about putting ice in the glasses?"

"I'm good at that," Mary Kate called cheerfully as she headed for the sink to wash her hands.

"Did you feel funny about that?" Sue asked casually.

Mary Kate frowned, unable to follow the woman's question. "Funny about. . .?" Her eyebrows rose questioningly.

"About being led up to see a picture of Mrs. Taylor."

Mary Kate looked across at Sue, sensing a friend in this woman, although she had wondered at times. "Awkward might be a better word. But. . .she was a very beautiful woman."

Sue opened the drawer of silverware and reached for a

serving spoon. "She was that, but she was a bit difficult, if I say so, which I probably shouldn't."

"Difficult?" Mary Kate paused at the refrigerator.

"Well, what I mean is. . ." she hesitated as though unsure what she did mean. She thrust the serving spoon into the casserole and glanced cautiously toward the open door. "She had lived a very privileged life in Memphis," she lowered her voice. "Her family always had servants and sometimes she made me feel as though I never quite measured up." She shook her head, lowering her eyes. "Shame on me for saying such a thing about the poor woman. She suffered terribly in the end."

Mary Kate nodded, opening the refrigerator door and reaching for the ice compartment. "I'm sure she did."

"The thing was," Sue continued in her confidential tone, "she was even more difficult during her illness. There were times when I didn't see how poor Mr. Taylor could endure her tantrums."

The words shocked Mary Kate as she attempted to drop ice cubes into tall crystal glasses.

"I'm sure he loved her very much," Mary Kate said quietly.

Sue hesitated. "He loved her in the beginning, but before she got sick, when she complained so much about living here, I think something happened between them. The week before she was diagnosed with cancer, I heard her ask for a divorce."

Mary Kate caught her breath at that bit of news.

Sue sighed and plunged on. "After she got sick, Mr. Taylor did everything he could to please her. Whatever she wanted, he got for her. But the illness progressed so fast. She was gone within three months after she was diagnosed. I felt sorry for her, but she became more difficult than ever."

Mary Kate realized they were gossiping about a woman who could no longer defend herself and felt ashamed to be participating. She glanced at Sue. "I'd rather not discuss this," she said gently.

Sue nodded. "And I should bite my tongue off. I guess the reason I'm saying these things to you is because I saw how Mr. Taylor acted when you were here, like he was happy for the first time in a very long while. And he was really disappointed that you couldn't join them today."

Mary Kate hesitated, tempted to tell Sue the truth, while knowing that was the last thing she should do. Then Sue surprised her even more with her next remark.

"I wanted to testify in the trial but Mr. Taylor wouldn't let me. Said he didn't want to subject me to the publicity."

Mary Kate turned quickly to face her, dropping an ice cube in the process. "What would you have said? In the trial, I mean."

Sue hesitated, reaching into the refrigerator for a tossed salad. "I'm not to discuss it. I promised Mr. Taylor. But believe me," she said, looking Mary Kate squarely in the eye, "he was innocent of those charges against him."

Mary Kate nodded, realizing that she believed this woman completely. She wondered why Blake had not allowed her to testify. Maybe he was confident of his defense, and as she had pointed out, he wanted to protect his housekeeper against more publicity.

At that moment, Hanna bounded into the room dressed in her play clothes.

"Can't you stay a while?" she asked, tugging at Mary Kate's hand.

As Mary Kate looked down into the little girl's pleading eyes, she almost gave in. "Hey, we're having lunch together, aren't we? And I eat slowly," she teased as the three women headed into the dining room.

"I had hoped my husband would join us," Sue was saying as they took their seats. "He got busy fixing our lawn mower and wouldn't come over, even though I've begged him not to mow our lawn on Sunday. . ."

While Sue droned on, Mary Kate's mind lingered on the startling news she had just been told, trying to digest everything at once.

It was Hanna who interrupted Sue's rambling with a very sensible plea. "Aren't we going to say a prayer? My Sunday school teacher said we should always thank God for our food."

"That's right," Mary Kate smiled at Hanna. "Want me to volunteer to say grace?"

Hanna nodded and Mary Kate offered a simple prayer. When she finished and glanced at Sue, the older woman looked embarrassed.

"I'm afraid I've failed miserably in that area," she said, picking up a linen napkin.

"We'll have to teach Dad to say a prayer before we eat," Hanna suggested brightly.

Sue nodded, passing the food. "I'm sure Mr. Taylor's mother always said grace at her table. Your dad has just gotten out of the habit."

Sue looked across at Mary Kate. "Mrs. Taylor is a lovely woman and a very religious one."

"She always makes me go to church with her when I visit," Hanna said, taking a large slurp of tea. Her blue eyes twinkled above her glass, and Mary Kate could see that she didn't mind going to church with her grandmother. "My other grandmother is different," Hanna frowned suddenly.

"They never say prayers. Neither did Mother."

Mary Kate cleared her throat. "Sue, this meal looks wonderful. How did you know I adore macaroni and cheese?"

"Because I do!" Hanna giggled.

The rest of the meal passed pleasantly with no more referrals to Charlotte Taylor or her family, and Mary Kate began to relax.

"Can't you just play one game of Monopoly before you go?"

Mary Kate hesitated, glancing at her watch. It was only one-fifteen. "If I remember correctly, a Monopoly game can last for hours."

Hanna shrugged. "We'll just play 'til you have to go. Please, Mary Kate. Please, please."

It was useless to refuse and Mary Kate knew it. After all, she had nothing else to do other than get ready for the coming week. And she really enjoyed being with Hanna.

"Okay. I'll play for a while but I need to leave in an hour or so."

"Great. Will you help me get the game?"

"Sure."

Sue was chuckling softly as she cleared the dishes. When she met Mary Kate's eyes, she gave her a warm smile. The woman was genuinely nice, and Mary Kate regretted feeling agitated with her the first time they met, after Hanna's disappearance. Now she understood that Sue was merely being protective of Hanna and she had every right to be.

They went back upstairs to Hanna's room where her games were neatly stacked on a shelf. The room was done in deep hues of pink with only a few pale pink touches. The furniture was cherry with a spindle post bed and matching dresser and bureau. The room was more formal than she would have chosen for a girl Hanna's age, Mary Kate thought, still, it was impressive.

"My goodness, look at all these games," Mary Kate said, placing her hands on her hips and shaking her head at Hanna. She was only teasing, of course, and Hanna knew it.

"Sue keeps them organized for me," Hanna boasted, happily taking no credit for the neat room. There was even a card table and four chairs placed beside the end window which overlooked a neat expanse of green lawn. It was a beautiful home, but again she felt that lonely quality that had touched her the first time she entered the house.

As Hanna laid out the board, Mary Kate began to stack the play money and line up the tiny hotels and cards. "You know I used to love to play this game," Mary Kate reminisced.

"You did?" Hanna glanced at her.

"Yep. My brother always beat me, but I just knew that one day I'd outsmart him." She laughed. "I never did."

"Dad's good at Monopoly," Hanna offered, concentrating on the board.

Mary Kate looked sharply at Hanna. Somehow it was difficult to imagine Blake Taylor hunkered down here at the table playing Monopoly with his daughter. She realized she had misjudged him when she once imagined that he spent no time with his daughter, that his life was his work.

She tried not to think about Blake or how she felt about him, as they began the game. An hour slipped away, and Mary Kate immediately realized what she had always suspected: Hanna had a very bright mind. Studying the little girl's blond head, tilted over the card she was drawing, Mary Kate found herself thinking of Charlotte. Hanna resembled her father more than her mother, and yet the delicacy that offset Blake's bolder features were gifts from mother to daughter. When finally she glanced at her watch and saw that it was two-thirty, she leaned back in the chair.

"Hanna, I hate to say so, but I really do have to leave now."

"Thank you for playing with me," Hanna beamed. Mary Kate had expected her to complain. To her surprise, Hanna seemed to realize it as she added, "Dad said I must behave better if I wanted to have you come visit us again."

Those words touched Mary Kate, bringing a tightness to her throat. "Well, you have behaved very well," she said tightly, coming to her feet. "Now I'll help you put the game away."

They began putting everything away, then suddenly Hanna frowned. "I need that little cup I always used to hold my hotels."

"Okay, where is it?"

She frowned. "I don't know. I haven't seen it since the last time Dad and I played."

"When was that?" Mary Kate asked helpfully,

Hanna was staring into space, thinking. "It was when Mom was really sick. Oh I know. He borrowed it to put something in for Mom." She leapt to her feet. "Come on, you may have to reach it for me."

Mary Kate trailed reluctantly along, uncomfortable at the prospect of trespassing in Blake's bedroom again. They entered his bedroom and Hanna ran to the closet and flung open the doors where Blake's clothes were lined up neatly on hangers.

Hanna pointed to the shoe boxes overhead. "They kept things put away up here."

Feeling like an intruder, Mary Kate followed orders and pulled down one shoe box after another, but there were only shoes inside the boxes.

Hanna frowned, looking around. "Mom was always look-ing for containers for her pills." She opened a bedside drawer, plunging around. At the back of the drawer, she found the cup. "Here it is!" She beamed at Mary Kate.

"Yep." Mary Kate removed a pill bottle from the cup for Hanna who had already turned on her heel to go. Mary Kate saw Charlotte's name on the label. As awkward as it would be taking it downstairs to Sue, she just couldn't leave it here within Hanna's reach, even though at eight Hanna was old enough to know better than to take them. Only a few small pills remained in the bottle—no, it was something else. Normally, she would not think to look in someone else's pill bottle, but she had glimpsed something through the amber plastic that aroused her curiosity.

Glancing at Hanna who was walking out of the room, Mary Kate quickly untwisted the bottle cap and peered inside. There at the very bottom of the bottle lay an exquis-ite ruby ring. Confused, she shook the ring into her palm without thinking. Charlotte had probably taken her ring off during her illness and placed it in the pill bottle when she was half asleep. And then she saw the tiny slip of paper encircling the silver band. *It's a price tag.* The numbers 1900 jumped at her. In her haste to replace the ring in the bottle, she almost dropped it. *Think Mary Kate. Wasn't there one piece of jewelry still missing?* With trembling fin-gers, she replaced the cap, shoved the bottle to the back of the drawer and closed the drawer.

Mary Kate stood trembling, staring at the drawer. Should she talk with Sue? Should she ask Blake? Should she call the police?

"Are you coming?" Hanna had returned to the doorway, and was peering in at Mary Kate.

"On my way," Mary Kate said shakily. Her mind was spinning in all directions, but she knew she must keep her cool until she got home. Only then would she be able to sit down and digest what she had just discovered.

Somehow she managed to gracefully thank Sue for lunch and quickly left the house. She drove home staring blankly at the traffic, numb with shock. But beneath the shock she knew there were questions simmering in the back of her mind, questions that must be answered.

O God, she prayed, *what am I going to do? Please, please show me the way.*

eleven

Somehow she managed to drive home without having an accident, park her car, and stumble into the safety of her apartment. Once inside, she felt her knees start to shake and she fell onto the sofa, her mind still half-frozen in shock. But the seclusion of her apartment gave her security, and now she curled up, hugging a pillow, trying to reason out what she had discovered.

The main question hammering at her now was: *what was she going to do?* She knew she would ask herself this a million times, but only God could give her the right answer.

She had found a ring, a valuable ring, one that had obviously been stolen. Or maybe Blake had purchased it for Charlotte and she had never taken the tag off. But why not keep it in a jewelry box? Why hide it in a pill bottle?

She blinked, trying to clear her muddled thoughts as her eyes moved slowly across the room and settled on her desk. *Clippings. Newspaper clippings.* Shakily, she got up, crossed the room to her desk, and opened the bottom drawer. She clipped and saved all the articles that were newsworthy in order to keep herself well-informed, and there was always the chance for a follow-up story in the future.

She sorted through several manila envelopes and finally retrieved the one labeled "The Taylor story." Gathering up the envelope of clippings, she recalled at one point being tempted to throw them out. The aftermath of her interview with Blake had been so bad that she didn't think she would have any desire to conduct a follow-up interview. But she had saved the clippings, prompted by some reason she hadn't quite understood. Had God been acting in her life even then, seeing her future, knowing this moment would someday come? Had He, in His infinite wisdom, known she would be forced to face a truth that would hurt her deeply? And yet she must face the truth.

Scolding Bo for getting underfoot, she made her way to the kitchen table where she could spread out the clippings. She was still wearing heels and her church dress, but she couldn't bother to change. The clippings were more important to her than anything else at the moment.

Carefully, she sorted through each one until she found what she was looking for: the article that detailed the stolen items. The one thing that was never recovered was. . .*a ruby ring,* and Blake Taylor claimed to have no knowledge of that, just as he reiterated that he had not taken any of the other valuable pieces.

She sat back in the kitchen chair, staring blindly into space. She felt as though she held the key to a secret door, but she had no idea what to do with the key. What, in good conscience, could she do? Tell the truth and destroy Blake and Hanna? Hide the truth and live with her scolding conscience? Her eyes strayed toward the phone. She knew the number of the district attorney's office for she had often called it in getting news.

The clock on the kitchen wall ticked into the silence that imprisoned her, the awful minutes of being held in the grip of indecision.

She turned and looked again at the clippings, trying to analyze her next move. She reminded herself that the trial was over now, old news. What good would it do to rehash the nightmare? After all, Blake had been acquitted. All she had to do was just forget about the ring she had found.

She closed her eyes, feeling miserable. Could she do that? Could she go against everything she had believed in all of her life? Could she live with herself if she did?

Her thoughts turned to Blake, and the love she thought she had felt for him. Tears filled her eyes. Had she been that blind to the man's true nature? Was their relationship a part of his game of deception? She couldn't believe that was true. She just wouldn't believe it.

But how could he do such a thing? she wondered, her mind bumping the stone wall of logic. Why would he steal items he could afford to purchase? *Or could he afford those items?* she wondered suddenly. Again, she plunged into the articles, sifting through them, rereading certain ones to refresh her memory. One of the motives for the robberies, according to the prosecution, was that Blake Taylor was deeply in debt. He had been in the process of changing insurance companies when his wife was diagnosed with cancer. None of her medical bills were covered. And the bills were staggering. Numerous hospitalizations, two surgeries, radiation treatments, a host of doctors' bills. What did Blake do under such staggering circumstances?

Sick at heart, Mary Kate carefully folded each article and replaced everything in the envelope. She had a sudden sickening impulse to toss them all in the trash, but she wanted to keep them. She must. This would serve as another reminder to her that she could never be involved with Blake Taylor. She knew that now. Brad had been right to warn her away.

Sue had said he would do anything to please Charlotte toward the end. No doubt, Charlotte was accustomed to the finer things in life, and Mary Kate could well imagine she would have collected valuable jewelry. *But why resort to theft?* she wondered miserably. Why didn't he sell something valuable to pay his bills? The house. No, of course he would not sell the house with his wife dying inside. The furniture? No. His most logical choice would be to work harder than ever to pay off his bills, and that was precisely what he had done. Everyone called him a workaholic. Even Hanna had hinted that her father had placed work above all else after her mother died. It had seemed a cruel thing for a grieving father to do, but now Mary Kate understood why. The man was desperate. Then, after Hanna had attempted to run away, the scare had forced him back into his fatherly role again.

Tears filled her eyes and rolled down her cheeks while Bo nestled at her feet, pretending to understand her depression. The entire situation was heartbreaking. Still, what he had done was wrong.

Thou shalt not steal. It was a commandment by which she had been reared. If Blake's mother was religious, no doubt he had been taught that commandment as well. But he was desperate, her heart argued. His wife was dying. The medical bills were staggering. Could he really be condemned for resorting to almost anything to bring a smile to Charlotte's face knowing she would soon be gone?

Thou shalt not steal. . . .

Reaching for a paper towel, she mopped the tears from her face and tried to force herself to think clearly. She could still see Hanna and she would. Her most important mission was to see that Hanna became a Christian, but she would do that and somehow manage to avoid Blake. Hadn't she done so today?

She came to her feet shakily, forcing herself back to her bedroom to undress. Rather than go to the mall to select a few outfits for her new job, she pulled on a nightshirt and crawled into bed, turning off the telephone. She had no desire to shop, to talk, to see anyone. Something inside her had wilted and died. And she knew what it was. She had fallen in love with Blake, against her better judgment, against Brad's advice. But that was exactly what she had done. And now she was forced to nurse a broken heart as she would have a physical ailment. Only this one hurt much worse.

❧

The pressure of a hectic Monday morning did nothing to improve Mary Kate's dark mood as she attempted to bury herself in work.

Carey popped through the door with a fresh cup of coffee. "I must say, you don't look like the happy news anchor everyone expected. Are you feeling ill?"

Mary Kate drew a deep breath and looked at her. "Just a bit. I guess I'm fighting off a virus, but I'll be okay. Thanks for the coffee. I needed it."

She hadn't slept more than three hours, and now she was dreadfully unprepared to face the busy week ahead. She managed to drag through the endless hours, poring over every news report. Then she sank into Annie's chair for her touch of magic before going on for the evening news.

"What are those dark circles doing under your eyes?" Annie frowned down at her.

"I'm fighting off a virus," she said, using the same excuse that had worked with Carey.

"Listen, girl, you better double up on the vitamins. This is no time to even think about getting sick."

"I know," Mary Kate sighed.

She could hardly believe her bad luck. Just when she needed to look her best, she looked her worst. Just when she should be feeling on top of the world, she felt as though she had lead in her shoes. All because of Blake. She bit her lip, hoping desperately she wouldn't start blubbering. That was all she needed, a crying jag just before she co-anchored the news for countless viewers.

"Here," Annie sat a cup of tea before her. "You need a dose of herbal tea and a vitamin." She uncapped a bottle and placed one beside the tea.

Mary Kate's eyes lingered on the innocent bottle of vitamins, but she was seeing again the pill bottle she had discovered only twenty-four hours ago, the bottle that had nailed Blake to the wall, as far as she was concerned.

"Now what's wrong?" Annie asked, the hairbrush poised in midair.

She shook her head. "Nothing." She took the vitamin and drank the tea and did, indeed, start to feel a bit better.

❀

By Wednesday Mary Kate's spirits were still low, but they plummeted when she studied a news report.

"Look at this!" She waved the report at Mr. Lucas who was sauntering past her desk. "There's a terrific story here, but we're only touching the surface."

He reached for the report, scanning its contents. "A high school student saves a woman from her burning home. How noble."

"But it's far more than noble, Mr. Lucas. Look at that last line," she pointed. "When the reporter asked him how it felt to be a hero, he said he just did what anyone else would have done. Don't you think that's absolutely remarkable coming from a sixteen-year-old who was running late for school?"

Mr. Lucas lifted an eyebrow and stared at her for a moment. "Why. . .yes. It is quite remarkable." He turned to go.

"But Mr. Lucas," she persisted, "why doesn't someone interview this boy for a special?" She glanced over the report he had handed back to her. "He risked his life. I think he deserves more recognition than his name and age, don't you?"

Mr. Lucas glanced back over his shoulder. "I'll tell Brad. In the meantime, Ms. Moore, I think you should remember that you're now an anchor, not an on-the-street reporter."

She glared after him, her cheeks flaming with anger. Then she slumped in her chair, staring again at the report, incensed that nobody was giving this boy the recognition he deserved.

"Cool it," Carey whispered as she darted by.

"I don't feel like cooling it!" Mary Kate called after her, not bothering to lower her voice. "When there's some sense-less murder, we give the bad guy prime time. When a young boy risks his life, we dismiss it with some flippant good-for-you remark and crowd the story into forty-five seconds. I don't like that, Carey." Her voice rose indignantly.

"Will you settle down?" Brad's sharp words spun her around, and she was looking straight into his icy stare. "You'd better control your tongue, little lady," he warned, spinning on his heel and taking off.

Mary Kate glared after him for a second, then pressed her lips tightly together, determined not to blow up. She took a deep breath and quietly accepted the cool soda Carey placed before her. Sipping it in silence, it occurred to her that she was walking a tightrope these days, torn with conflict over Blake on one side, and struggling with a new job she didn't like on the other.

Her eyes sneaked toward the closed doors of Mr. Lucas's office. How could she possibly have presumed to tell Mr. Lucas how to run the station? Even Brad would never do that.

She took another sip of the cool drink then placed it on her desk. Trying to dredge up some enthusiasm for her evening report, she picked up the typewritten pages. And then she knew exactly what was wrong. She missed her interviews, that was it. She missed the opportunity to pursue a Christian approach to news reporting. As she analyzed her feelings, she realized she missed her rapport with the man on the street. Interviewing people had been her main source of enjoyment, particularly people who were an inspiration to others—like the handicapped artist who had been the object of one interview. That interview had ended up gaining national recognition for the artist. When she went home that night, she felt she had accomplished something.

But this—she stared miserably at the news she would deliver this evening. This was not for her. She only thought she wanted to be an anchor, but now she hated everything about it: worrying about a wardrobe of fashionable clothes, the right cosmetics, the best hairstyle. Just this morning, Brad had pointed out that a female anchor must be pretty enough to win public approval, but not too pretty to detract from the news she was delivering.

Her eyes lifted to the can of soda, and she realized she hadn't eaten since breakfast. In fact, she had scarcely touched her meals since. . .Sunday.

Again, the memory of the ruby ring dragged at her. It was becoming apparent to her that she could not just sweep this under her mental rug. She had to deal with it. Even if it meant a long talk with Sue—or even confronting Blake.

She just couldn't live with this. It was making her ill.

Just then Brad swept by her desk again and she knew what she had to do.

"Brad, could I speak with you for a minute?"

twelve

"You *what?*"

"I want to give up the anchor job and go back to my on-the-street interviews."

He stared at her as though she had slapped him. "I can't believe you're saying this, Mary Kate. Do you honestly know what you're doing?"

She nodded her head. "I honestly do. I'm miserable."

He leaned back in his chair, his arms crossed over his chest. "I don't know what Mr. Lucas is going to say."

She sighed. "If it's a major problem, I'll just resign."

"Resign?" he echoed, more shocked than ever.

"Brad, first you tell me how to run my personal life. Then—"

"So that's it!" He glared at her suspiciously.

"That's only part of it. I could still handle that request if I were happy at work. But I'm not. If I can't go back to the job I had before, I'm leaving."

It occurred to her that maybe she should be leaving anyway. She wasn't sure she could stay in the same town with Blake and Hanna.

"Tell you what," Brad said, his tone more logical, "do the evening newscast, then take tomorrow off and think about what you're doing. I'm sure we can still call the guy in Jacksonville and offer him the job. He really wanted it. Mr. Lucas just favored you." He grinned. "And so did I."

"Well, Mr. Lucas may not look so favorably upon me now," she said with a deep sigh.

Brad pursed his lips. "Let me talk to him. And as I suggested—take tomorrow off and clear your head."

She nodded. "I have something I need to take care of anyway."

He tilted his head and looked at her strangely, but wisely asked her nothing more.

જ

After the newscast she felt as though a load had been lifted from her shoulders, and as she drove home, she felt far more equipped to deal with her personal problems. And she *had* to deal with them, she knew that much.

She drove into the driveway, cut the engine, and hopped out of the car. Once she had unlocked her door and stopped in the living room to pet Bo, she went to the kitchen, determined to eat a sensible meal for the first time all week. She had been existing on sandwiches and microwave dinners, only half touched. Her stomach had rolled over at the thought of food. In all honesty, her stomach had not felt right since she found the ruby ring.

She took a deep breath. She would deal with that later. She decided on bacon and eggs, canned biscuits, and honey, a supper her mother often fixed on cold winter nights. She hesitated, thinking of her mother. For a moment, she almost called her to discuss the situation with her. Maybe she would even ride up to Dothan in the morning to talk things out with her. Her mother had that marvelous ability of seeing both sides of a problem and solving it sensibly.

Just then the phone rang. She finished washing her hands under the kitchen faucet and dried them with a towel.

Her merry hello caught in her throat at the sound of Blake's voice on the other end.

"Have I called at a bad time?" he asked.

"No." She took a deep breath and sent a silent prayer winging toward the heavens. "In fact I'm glad you called."

"Oh? What's up?"

"For starters, I've resigned as anchor. I'm going back to my on-the-street interviews."

"You are?" He didn't really sound surprised at her announcement.

"You're much more calm than my boss was about my decision."

"Because I understand why. You have a special talent with your interviews. A creativity. There's not that much creativity in being an anchor, is there?"

She smiled, relieved that someone had voiced what she hadn't been quite able to pinpoint. "That's exactly right."

"Then I'm happy for you."

She took a deep breath and plunged in. "Blake, there's more. As a matter of fact, I really must talk with you as soon as possible."

"You sound awfully serious."

"Yes, I am."

"Want me to come over?"

She shook her head. She wasn't ready to deal with this tonight. "I'm sure your schedule is filled tomorrow, but I've taken the day off to straighten some things out. Is there any way you could meet me for lunch?"

"I can do better than that. It so happens my eleven o'clock appointment canceled, and I'll have a couple of hours free, so we're in luck. Where do you want to meet?"

She thought it over. "Could I come to your house? It's quieter there, and what I have to say is private."

"You're beginning to worry me, Mary Kate. But sure, we can meet here at the house. I'll have Sue prepare a lunch for us."

"Fine."

"Mary Kate?"

"Yes?"

"Are you thinking of leaving Seabreeze?"

"I'm not sure. There's a possibility I might."

"Then we definitely need to talk. I don't want you to go." His tone was warm and caring and Mary Kate felt a rush of tears to her eyes.

She had to get off the phone before she started blubbering. "Okay, we'll talk. Now I really need to run. I have several things to do." She knew her voice sounded more formal, but she wanted to keep it that way. She had to be formal with him until she knew the truth. And then there was the possibility that she might be saying good-bye to him. Forever.

❧

When she drove into the Taylor driveway the next morning, her memory returned to her first visit here, when she had come out of concern for Hanna. The relationship between father and daughter had certainly changed since then, but she would not let herself think about how it was going to hurt once she left the house for good. Maybe there was a reasonable answer, or maybe she would never know the real truth. But she had to try and find out, or things could never be the same between her and Blake.

His car was already in the driveway, and again she voiced a silent prayer for strength. This was one of the toughest things she had ever had to do in her entire life, and she wondered if she could even go through with it. But she knew she had to. It was unfair to Blake not to give him a chance to explain.

She glanced one last time in the mirror. She had dressed conservatively in a navy pants suit, with little makeup.

She tried to tell herself this was a business meeting and to approach it in that manner. In her heart of hearts, she knew her entire world was turning on what happened here this morning. Again, she told herself, she had to know the truth.

She reached for her shoulder bag and got out. As she approached the front steps, the door swung back, and Blake was standing there, still dressed in a business suit minus a tie. His pale blue shirt was unbuttoned, giving him a more casual appearance, and with the blue accenting his brown hair and blue eyes, her heart gave a lurch.

She dropped her eyes to the top step, determined to keep her guard up.

"Good morning," he called. "Although I must admit the look on your face doesn't quite say good morning."

"Good morning," she said, forcing a half-smile.

As she entered she could smell Sue's delicious meal, but Blake took her arm and ushered her into the den. "Sue said it's going to be another fifteen minutes before the chicken is done, so we can talk first, if that's okay."

She nodded. "That's fine."

Once they were settled quietly in the den, with the door closed, Blake studied her face carefully. He was obviously eager to hear what she had to say.

She looked at him, saying nothing for a moment. More than anything she had ever done in her life, she hated to say what she had come to say. Or to ask.

"Can I help you get started?" he prompted, suddenly looking serious. "It's obviously hard for you to begin. Does it have to do with me?"

She nodded her head and took a deep breath.

"Shall we play sixty-four questions? Want me to start guessing?"

She shook her head and lowered her eyes, fidgeting with the strap of her shoulder bag. "Blake, I have to know the truth about something." She looked up at him. "And I pray you will be honest with me."

His eyes darkened. "Of course I'll be honest with you, Mary Kate. I always have been. What in the world is it?"

She took a deep breath and lifted her eyes to the ceiling. "I was playing Monopoly with Hanna Sunday and she was missing her little cup. The one that holds the hotels."

He nodded, clearly confused about where this was leading.

"She said it might be in your room, that sometimes your wife kept the cup for her pill bottles."

She watched him carefully, trying to read a difference in his expression, but it did not change.

"Hanna found the cup in the back of the top drawer of your nightstand. It held a pill bottle. I was going to bring the bottle down to Sue—for Hanna's safety—when I noticed. . .a ring in it." She lowered her eyes for a moment then looked at him again. She could see that he was beginning to understand where this was leading. "It was a ruby ring with the price tag still attached. The one ring that was never recovered from the theft."

He heaved a sigh and leaned back in the chair. "And so you think I did steal the jewelry and just forgot about the ruby ring."

"I don't know what to think," she replied honestly.

He pursed his lips and looked across the room at her. "Then you deserve to know the truth."

She waited, her breath bated.

"Charlotte took the jewelry."

"Charlotte?" she echoed, astounded by that bit of information. "But she was sick, she—"

"She felt that being hit with cancer at such a young age was unfair. She became unreasonable, demanding. I spent thousands of dollars on clothes she never wore. Then something changed. It was as if she needed to extend the cruel game she was playing to someone beyond this household. She suddenly began wanting to go jewelry shopping two weeks before she died."

He paused, took a deep breath. "I had exhausted most of my funds on her care by that time, but I still had a little space on my charge card. We went to the jewelry store she liked so much. She was in a wheelchair by then, and we moved from counter to counter. At the expensive counter, she lingered, wanting to look at everything. The salesgirl saw her condition and was very helpful, taking out various expensive items. Charlotte suggested I go over to the front counter and pick up a charm bracelet for Hanna, and I did. I put the item on my charge card and returned to where Charlotte was talking with the salesgirl.

"I noticed the girl seemed upset, because Charlotte had been cross with her, demanding to see more and more items. The poor girl took pity on Charlotte, seeing her condition. While I was away, Charlotte had apparently pocketed several items, then closed the case and returned it to the salesgirl, so the girl did not argue; she was trying desperately to please her.

"Amazingly, she got away with it. Then Charlotte sent me to another counter to look for something for her mother, and while I was gone the salesgirl noticed what Charlotte was doing. She discreetly suggested Charlotte take the jewelry out of her pocket or give her a hundred dollars." He shook his head. "Naturally, Charlotte gave her some money, for she was getting quite a bargain with the jewelry she had stashed in her pocket. As for the scarf and the designer bag, she must have picked those up the same day when we went to a department store just down the street. She was always having me get her water or do something for her. She seemed to enjoy having me wait on her."

He sighed, dropping his head to his hands. "Then, there was a break-in which was for real, but the only thing taken was the VCR near the door because the police arrived just before the burglar made his getaway. The next week, when the jewelry store inventoried their items, they discovered the missing pieces. After checking the sales slips and credit cards, they interviewed everyone who had been in the shop that day. Of course I knew nothing about the missing jewelry, but Charlotte did. She enjoyed taking the expensive pieces out when she was alone, looking at them, perhaps imagining how life could have been or how it was when she was younger and her parents bought her everything she wanted."

He took a deep breath as though hating to continue, but as his eyes slipped over Mary Kate's face, he forced himself to finish the story. "I was out of town on the day the detective came to the house. When he questioned Charlotte, he detected that she was lying by the way she answered the questions. She was bedfast by then, and thinking she could not have stolen the jewelry herself, they suspected me. He got a search warrant of the house. They were thorough—they found everything but the ring. And now I'll see that it's returned."

When he had finished Mary Kate sat staring at him, weighing out what he had said. "But why didn't you—?"

"Why didn't I tell the truth about it all? The trauma of what had happened made Charlotte worse. She died two days later.

On the day before she died, she told me what she had done and why, and she begged me never to tell Hanna. Somehow I couldn't bring myself to go to the district attorney."

"I can understand you were upset, and yet if you had told them the truth. . ."

"Well, of course there was the funeral which occupied all of us. We had out-of-town guests, and Hanna was distraught. The next week, when the detective called again, I made a decision to avoid telling him for two reasons: one, because I couldn't bear to sully Charlotte's reputation, and two, it may have looked like I was blaming my late wife to save my own skin. I preferred to fight the charges with a good lawyer rather than having Hanna know her mother became a thief. Her parents would never have believed she did it. They always defended her. That was one of the problems—she was very spoiled and pampered. I imagine they would have gone to court to get custody of Hanna if I had said Charlotte took the jewelry. Everyone would have been convinced that I did it, anyway."

A knock sounded on the door.

"Come in."

Sue entered, nodding a hello to Mary Kate.

"Lunch is ready."

"Sue, I want you to tell Mary Kate what you would have testified in court."

She looked stunned for a moment, then glancing from Blake to Mary Kate she walked across the room and settled into a chair.

"I overheard part of a conversation between Mrs. Taylor and the salesgirl from the jewelry store. The girl came here, looking upset, wanting to see Mrs. Taylor. I couldn't help overhearing bits and pieces of the conversation after I left the room and started down the hall. Mrs. Taylor was saying something about paying her more money. The girl said she wanted to go back to Texas. When I told Mr. Taylor about this, it was already too late. The police had been here asking questions, the jewelry had been returned, and Mrs. Taylor was so ill, then. He didn't want to retract what he had already told them, but he had nothing to do with the theft. That's the truth."

Mary Kate looked from Sue to Blake, her eyes filling with tears. How could she have doubted him? Why didn't she trust her heart enough to know she could not love a deceptive man? That this man was a wonderful father, had tried to be a good husband. Her eyes locked with his as she tried to verbalize all that filled her heart.

"I can't tell you how relieved I am—and how sorry I am for doubting you, Blake." Mary Kate swallowed back tears of regret and sympathy. Blake had been through so much, it didn't seem fair for one person to have to endure what he had. Yet, he had not taken the easy road out. He had put his daughter first, even his wife, despite her cruel treatment of him. *How can I ever make up to him for doubting him?* Mary Kate wondered.

Now, looking into his tormented eyes, she wanted more than anything in the world to help him find happiness again. The room was very quiet as both Sue and Blake watched her, and she knew she must lighten the mood before they all started crying.

"Well Sue," she brightened, "for the first time in days, my appetite has returned and something in that kitchen smells absolutely divine."

"I'll go finish up then," Sue said, forcing a smile while casting a concerned glance toward Blake as she left the room.

Blake walked across the room and extended his hand, lifting Mary Kate up from the chair. "You've been carrying a terrible load, haven't you?"

"Not like the one you carried. Oh, Blake, this whole thing must have been horrible for you."

He sighed. "It was. And it would have been worse if I had been convicted. I just kept praying that my innocence would win out. I really knew nothing of any of it until Charlotte told me when she was dying. She admitted what she had done and begged me never to tell Hanna."

He hesitated, running a broad hand across his head as though the memory had stirred up a terrible headache. When he spoke again, his voice was low and quiet. "It was the day after the salesgirl came. When I questioned Sue, she obviously didn't know what to do. She hadn't been certain she had heard the conversation right, but she was sure of one thing: Charlotte had given the girl money. After I explained to her what Charlotte had told me, then she was certain her ears weren't playing tricks on her. Charlotte had taken the jewelry."

He closed his eyes for a moment, as though a wave of pain had crashed over him. "What would *you* do under those circumstances, Mary Kate? The store had the jewelry back, so all that was left was to fight the charges and the press, and try to live down the accusation against me."

She considered his words, wondering what she would have done. Given the circumstances, she wasn't sure she could have been as protective as he had been. But she knew one thing for sure: Blake Taylor had done what he believed was best.

"You did what you thought was the right thing for your little girl, Blake."

He nodded slowly as his eyes drifted over her head to gaze out the window. "I really think Charlotte's mind was affected toward the end. She had a tumor at the brain stem that was inoperable. Most people who are diagnosed with that condition live at least six months, sometimes longer. She only made it for three months."

"Oh Blake," Mary Kate said, putting her arms around him, "how could I ever have doubted you?"

"Because you have a head full of common sense. Why wouldn't you doubt me?"

As they looked into each others eyes, Blake lowered his lips to hers in a sweet warm kiss. Her hands moved up his shoulders and fastened around his neck as he pulled her against his chest and kissed her again.

"Iced tea?" Sue called from down the hall.

Mary Kate broke away laughing. "We'd better go."

"Before we do, there's something else I need to say. I'm in love with you, Mary Kate."

She gasped as tears rose to her eyes. "And I love you, Blake. I have almost from the beginning."

He kissed her again; then hand in hand, they walked out of the den and down the hall to the kitchen.

"Mary Kate, I think maybe I should go back and have another talk with Hal Traina, the district attorney," Blake said, studying the carpet as they walked into the dining room.

Mary Kate stopped walking and looked at him. "Why?"

He sighed. "Because Hanna wants to become a Christian and I want to rededicate my life. I think it's important to clear all dishonesty out of my past. Maybe I should have told the truth all along."

"You did tell the truth. You were innocent."

"But I knew what had really happened."

Mary Kate stared into his eyes, worried. "But Blake, this could mean they'll drag you back through the press again and—"

"They may," he agreed. "But I feel it's important that I clear my conscience. Then it will be up to the district attorney to decide what to do."

She nodded slowly. In her heart, she was relieved that he was making this decision. It was the right thing to do, even though he had promised Charlotte he wouldn't tell. Still, it was unfair for him to live his life under a cloud of suspicion.

"Then I'm going down there with you, Blake. This time I won't let you face that agony alone."

thirteen

The next morning Mary Kate and Blake sat together in District Attorney Hal Traina's office behind closed doors. Sue had accompanied them, prepared to give a deposition, or do whatever was required of her. Blake wanted everything out in the open now. The district attorney had called in the assistant district attorney and the lead investigator. All had been alerted something important was about to be discussed.

Blake began to tell the story, slowly, methodically, each event unfolding in a logical manner. Mary Kate watched the men in the room, wondering why they wouldn't believe him. After all, the truth made more sense than anything else. Shock then disbelief seized their features, and occasionally they exchanged glances but no one spoke or asked a single question until he had finished.

For several seconds, there was complete silence in the room. Then Hal Traina looked at Sue. "And you are prepared to give a deposition to what you overheard?"

"I am. And it's more than just overhearing the conversation, sir. The girl came to our house, I opened the door, and led the way up to Mrs. Taylor's bedroom."

"We can make a charge against the girl and you, Mrs. Sampson, for withholding information," the assistant district attorney spoke up.

"May I say one more thing?" Sue asked, clearly not intimidated by any of the men. "Mrs. Taylor threatened the girl.

She told her she would deny everything and see that she lost her job. She threw some bills toward the girl, but I cannot testify for sure that she took the money. I do know that she was threatened. It was not clear to me what Mrs. Taylor would deny until later when she admitted taking the jewelry."

The men exchanged long meaningful glances and the district attorney sighed and shook his head.

"Taylor, you've really complicated our lives, you know that? I'm curious as to why you came to tell us this now. You know we can't try you again for the same crime. And all the jewelry has been returned."

"Except for a ruby ring we found yesterday." He removed it from his pocket, still in Charlotte's pill bottle. "Shall I return it to the store or let you take it?"

The three men exchanged shocked glances as they realized what they had put this man through. "We'll take it to the jeweler and explain this to them. But you still haven't answered my question. This case is finally dying down in the public eye. Why would you want to risk stirring things up again?"

"Believe me, sir, for the sake of my daughter, the last thing I want to do is dredge up that story again. But my daughter wants to give her heart to God, and so do I. And I happen to have fallen in love with a wonderful woman," he looked at Mary Kate, who squeezed his hand. "It doesn't help her reputation for people to think she is seeing a man accused of stealing."

The district attorney shifted uncomfortably in his chair and cast a swift glance around the room. The other men had dropped their heads.

"You've done a remarkable thing for your daughter. And yourself. And these women," the district attorney looked from Blake to Sue to Mary Kate. "I must say I have enormous respect for you all for coming in here today."

Blake smiled weakly. "Thank you."

"As for what you've just told us, give us some time to discuss this." He stood up, signaling that the discussion had ended. "Thank you for coming."

They shook hands, and Mary Kate noticed that all the men were looking at Blake with eyes that reflected their respect, as well.

Blake opened the door for Sue and Mary Kate and they walked quietly out of the complex of offices and down the corridor. No one spoke until they were outside in the fresh balmy air of a pleasant day in Seabreeze.

Sue turned and looked at Blake. "Now what do you think will happen?"

Blake shook his head. "I don't know. But I feel like I've just swallowed the glow of the sun." His eyes rested on Mary Kate and she looked up at him with love shining clearly in her brown eyes.

"Blake, I've never been so proud of anyone in my entire life," she said with tears shining in her brown eyes. "Too bad I have to get back to work."

He shrugged. "So do I. But it doesn't matter. I feel like the weight of the world just came off my shoulders! I feel great, darling. . ."

He leaned down and planted a quick kiss on her lips. "Now remember, we're going to my favorite restaurant tonight, and we're going to have a wonderful dinner over candlelight. And I'm going to whisper sweet nothings in your ears!"

She laughed. "I can't wait." They stared at each other for another long moment, then Mary Kate took a step back from him, forcing herself to say good-bye. "Tonight," she nodded. She turned and walked back to her car feeling as if she had wings on her feet and that she was floating rather than walking.

ða

When she arrived back at the WJAK office, the phones were ringing, as usual. Mary Kate took a deep breath, trying to orient herself as she studied the newsroom. Everyone looked busy. It didn't seem to matter to anyone that she was two hours late for work. As her eyes took in the stacks of papers on desks and the people attached to phones, it amused her to think that her life had changed drastically in the past weeks, and yet nobody really seemed to notice.

She took a seat at her desk and began sorting through her telephone messages. On her desk was one report in particular that interested her. She had been assigned to do a special on-the-street interview of the young high school student who had saved a woman from her burning home. The boy had agreed to the interview and Mary Kate was ecstatic.

At that moment, Coty entered the newsroom and she waved to him. "We have a great on-the-street interview," she handed him a copy of the report.

He read it over and grinned. "This is great." He laid the report back on her desk, still looking into her face, grinning. "I'm so glad to have you back working with me. And I have something to tell you, Mary Kate."

"What is it?" she asked, studying his face. "And don't make me guess, just tell me."

He leaned down, planting his large palms on her desk. "Sharon and I are back together again, Mary Kate. And I have you to thank for it."

"Back together?" she repeated, staring at him, wide-eyed. "Coty, that's wonderful." But then she was puzzled. "Why are you thanking me? I had nothing to do with it."

"The New Testament you gave me has made all the difference in the world," he said huskily. "I've been reading it, and I'm here to tell you those words have melted this hard heart of mine. I've been turned around from the old beer-guzzling, woman-chasing Coty!"

"I'm so happy for you, Coty!" she smiled brightly, studying the big man, so obviously changed.

"I'll bring your New Testament back in a few days. Sharon is reading it now."

"Coty," she reached forward, gripping his hand, "keep it as a wedding present. You will remarry, won't you?"

He nodded. "Right away. Well, I'd better scoot."

"Thanks for telling me this, Coty," she said, staring after him as he left the room. She sighed, feeling a surge of happiness for the divorced couple who belonged together. Then her eyes fell to the report and she tried to concentrate on her work again.

The interview—

She jumped up from her desk and barged into Brad's office before realizing he was having a private conversation on the telephone. She stepped outside his office and waited until he hung up, then she rushed back in.

"Brad, I'm sorry I burst in on you like that, but I'm so excited about this." She waved the report. "Thank you so much for allowing me to cover this story."

He grinned. "You were right. It is a good story. And now even Mr. Lucas thinks so."

She sank into the chair opposite him and took a deep breath. "Is he very upset with me about turning down the anchor job?"

Brad tilted his head and looked at her strangely. "You

know what he said to me? 'If we had more employees as dedicated to a job as Mary Kate Moore, WJAK could set a wonderful example for other stations.' " He shook his head, clearly dismayed. "I had expected him to be angry, but he wasn't. Which brings up another point."

He got up and crossed the room, closing the door.

Oh no, she thought, *another lecture about Blake*. She had made up her mind on that point also; if he made the same threat about her not seeing him, she was going to resign. As important as her job had seemed to her, she now realized that nothing was more important to her than Blake and Hanna, and everyone's relationship with God.

"I've just had a long talk with Mr. Lucas about you," he said, taking a seat behind the desk again.

"Oh?" she lifted her brow, waiting for the other shoe to drop.

"It seems that he and Hal Traina, the district attorney, are close friends. He has just enlightened me about some new information on the Blake Taylor case. It seems I owe you an apology, and I imagine all of Seabreeze owes Blake Taylor one, as well."

She gasped. "You know about Blake's meeting with the district attorney?" she asked, amazed that he had heard the news so quickly.

"Just as word of mouth did more to damage his reputation than anything else, I think Hal and his staff decided it would be appropriate if a bit of gossip was now passed along, revealing the truth of the matter. I gather there will be no more trials."

She took a deep breath and tried to hold onto her optimism. "I don't know what will happen. We just left his office this morning. I'm praying that everyone will come to realize what a good man Blake Taylor is."

"I trust your judgment, Mary Kate. After all, you are a people person; you know how to read people, and you were right about him. I owe you an apology."

"Thanks, Brad," she said smiling at him.

"Incidentally, I know you were with Taylor today. The district attorney is a very nice guy, actually, and apparently he sensed your delicate situation in the matter. He didn't want your job affected by idiots like me. I'm sorry, Mary Kate."

She leaned back in her chair, at a total loss for words. "I. . . It's okay, Brad. Just as long as people understand, everything is okay. In fact, it's wonderful."

Brad leaned across the desk, his voice lowered. "Are you in love with him?"

She hesitated only a moment, not because she was unsure of her feelings, but this was the first time she had admitted her love to anyone but Blake. "Yes, Brad," she said quietly. "I'm head over heels in love with him. And I think he feels the same way for me."

"Then let me be the first to wish you all the happiness in the world."

Tears filled her eyes. "Thanks, Brad. And I promise to do my job better than ever."

He nodded. "I'll be expecting that." He had lapsed back to his old teasing manner, breaking the emotional tension between them.

She stood, glancing again at the report. "Now I want to go make some notes on this story so I can do the interview justice."

She dashed out the door, her mind spinning with all that was happening. Last week she had been dragging the ground, and now, this week, she was soaring in the clouds.

fourteen

As she prepared for her date with Blake, she took the time for a leisurely soak in her favorite bath oil. So much had happened that it was hard for her to fathom it all. And yet she had always believed in miracles. Her problem was that she never gave God enough time to bring about those miracles.

She captured a clear bubble floating on the soothing suds. Why couldn't she ever get it through her head that God had His own way of working things out? And He always seemed to do things perfectly when given time. She sighed, sinking deeper into the bath water as she rested her head against the back of the tub.

"My problem," she said aloud, "is that I want to jump in and fix things myself. Maybe this time I've learned," she added softly, feeling a burst of joy in her heart as she thought of Blake and Hanna and the love they now shared.

She closed her eyes for a moment, inhaling the wonderful scent of cinnamon cake candle she enjoyed burning while she took her bath. Her mind drifted toward the evening's date with Blake. She knew exactly what she would wear. Over her lunch hour, she had gone into the boutique that had been beckoning to her for weeks. In the past, she kept walking past the boutique, forcing herself to be frugal. Today, however, she felt that a celebration was in order.

It had been wonderful to go inside the exclusive boutique and wander around the racks of dresses, looking for something that suited her mood. She found it quickly—a long flowing skirt of pale blue cotton with a sleeveless blue, silk blouse. When she took the outfit to the dressing room and tried it on, it looked as though it had been made for her. The sky-blue color accented her dark hair and eyes, and the soft sheer flow of fabric gave her the sensation of floating through the air. And in her heart, that was exactly what she felt she was doing.

Deliberately, she avoided looking at the price tag, knowing the years of frugal training her parents had instilled might now tempt her not to buy the outfit. She changed back to her other clothes and took the outfit to the counter. Then she spotted a pair of backless silver sandals.

"Those would be terrific with the dress," the young saleswoman assured her.

This was all the prompting she needed. Fortunately, the sandals came in her size, which she considered an omen. She added the shoes to the outfit then whipped out her charge card, ignoring the total figure.

"This is a lovely outfit," the woman said to her. "Are you going somewhere special?"

Mary Kate nodded. "Very special."

"Then I hope you enjoy your outfit."

Mary Kate smiled at her. "I'm sure I will."

Now, recalling the outfit, she forced herself out of the tub, rubbing down with a thick terry towel. She applied lotion and powder and pulled on a robe. Then she sat down before the mirror to concentrate on her face. Tonight, she would add a bit more makeup than usual, only a small bit. She had already shampooed her hair, but she still had time to touch it up.

Humming a love song to herself, she thought about calling her mother. It was definitely time to tell her about Blake. She and her mother had always been very close, and she wanted to deliver her good news. But as she stared into her sparkling brown eyes, she decided to wait and see what the coming days brought. And she wanted to see how she felt about Blake Taylor after tonight.

⁂

As it turned out, there was no point in worrying about the evening. It couldn't have gone better.

Blake arrived, wearing a soft tan sports coat and trousers in a chocolate brown. Beneath the coat, his shirt was a soft cream. She thought he had never looked more appealing.

He gave a low whistle when he saw her. "Well, hello."

She smiled up at him. "Hello to you. Want a glass of iced tea or something?"

He shook his head. "Let's allow ourselves enough time to enjoy the drive."

"Fine." Gathering her purse and locking the door, her hand slipped easily into his as they walked out to his car.

Soon they were out of the downtown traffic and onto the beach highway.

"I have a favorite restaurant near the house that I think you'll enjoy," he said above the soothing flow of a nice instrumental in his tape deck. "Funny, it's called Summer Place, and maybe that's how we started calling our beach house by that name. Anyway, I thought it was the perfect place for us to go for a celebration dinner."

She nodded, looking at him. "Sounds great."

He seemed to have dropped several years from his face, his hair was shining from a recent shampoo, and his blue eyes glowed with happiness as he turned into the restaurant parking lot and cut the engine.

He came around to open her door for her, and they got

out and walked up the steps to the quaint little restaurant, nestled on a quiet little strip of land hugging the ocean.

"We'd like a table by the window," he said to the hostess. "I called to request one earlier."

She recognized him and nodded. "We put down your request as soon as you called, Mr. Taylor."

Mary Kate glanced up at him, smiling. "So you called ahead."

"As soon as you said you could go."

The hostess led them to a table for two by a window that overlooked the sparkling blue water. It was a lovely evening, with the sun beginning to sink on the horizon, dropping a raspberry hue over the ocean.

Mary Kate took a deep breath and sighed. "How lovely."

She felt his hand gripping hers and she turned to face him.

"I'm so grateful for you, Mary Kate. I truly believe God put us together. I've thought a lot about what you said about how you had prayed for the right person." He took a deep breath. "I never did. I'm not saying anything against Charlotte. She was a good person."

Mary Kate nodded. "I know. When I look at Hanna, I realize that."

"What I'm saying is. . .well, I guess what I'm asking is if you think that. . ." his voice trailed, as he dropped his eyes to her fingers, entwined in his.

"If I think what?" she asked, squeezing his hand. Then she understood what he didn't seem to have the courage to ask. "If I think you're that man?" she asked tenderly. "Yes, Blake I do. Without a doubt."

His gaze reached into hers and for a moment there was a sheen of tears glazing the deep blue eyes. He sighed. "Mary

Kate, I'm in love with you, very much in love with you. I don't know what I ever did to deserve you, but I promise I'll spend the rest of my life trying to be the person you want me to be."

"Just be who God wants you to be, Blake. And you did that today."

He nodded. "And Sunday I will be joining you and Hanna. After all, we want to start our life together in the right way."

She nodded, feeling her throat tighten. Then suddenly she gave up, as tears began to trickle down her cheeks. "Oh Blake, I'm so happy."

The waitress stood at the table, staring at them, hating to interrupt.

"It's okay," Blake turned to her, grinning. "We just got engaged." He reached into his pocket and pulled out a small navy case.

Mary Kate's breath caught.

"I'll come back," the waitress said with a smile, discreetly slipping away.

He opened the tiny box and Mary Kate was looking at an exquisite solitaire that took her breath away. "Oh Blake, it's gorgeous. I don't know what to say."

"Just say yes," he said, slipping the ring onto her finger. It fit perfectly. "If there's another kind you'd rather have, we can go to the jewelry store after work tomorrow night. After all," he laughed, "I've become good friends with the manager."

"Is it the same one that—?" And then she was laughing too.

"Funny thing. He seemed really glad to see me."

Mary Kate nodded, thinking of what Brad had said about word getting around.

"This one suits me perfectly," she said. "Just like you."

They kissed then, not caring who saw them. All they cared about was that at last they had found true love during their darkest hour.

A Letter To Our Readers

Dear Reader:

In order that we might better contribute to your reading enjoyment, we would appreciate your taking a few minutes to respond to the following questions. When completed, please return to the following:

Rebecca Germany, Managing Editor
Heartsong Presents
PO Box 719
Uhrichsville, Ohio 44683

1. Did you enjoy reading *Summer Place?*
   - ❑ Very much. I would like to see more books by this author!
   - ❑ Moderately
     I would have enjoyed it more if _____

   _____

2. Are you a member of **Heartsong Presents**? ❑Yes ❑No
   If no, where did you purchase this book?_____

   _____

3. What influenced your decision to purchase this book? (Check those that apply.)

❑ Cover	❑ Back cover copy
❑ Title	❑ Friends
❑ Publicity	❑ Other_____

4. How would you rate, on a scale from 1 (poor) to 5 (superior), the cover design?_____

5. On a scale from 1 (poor) to 10 (superior), please rate the following elements.

    ___Heroine   ___Plot

    ___Hero   ___Inspirational theme

    ___Setting   ___Secondary characters

6. What settings would you like to see covered in **Heartsong Presents** books?_____

_____

_____

7. What are some inspirational themes you would like to see treated in future books?_____

_____

_____

8. Would you be interested in reading other **Heartsong Presents** titles? ❑ Yes   ❑ No

9. Please check your age range:
   ❑ Under 18   ❑ 18-24   ❑ 25-34
   ❑ 35-45   ❑ 46-55   ❑ Over 55

10. How many hours per week do you read? _____

Name _____

Occupation_____

Address_____

City_____ State_____ Zip_____

I Do

A Romantic Collection of Inspirational Novellas

Discover how two words, so softly spoken, create one glorious life with love's bonds unbroken. *I Do,* a collection of four all-new contemporary novellas from **Heartsong Presents** authors, will be available in May 1998. What better way to love than with this collection written especially for those who adore weddings. The book includes *Speak Now or Forever Hold Your Peace* by Veda Boyd Jones, *Once Upon a Dream* by Sally Laity, *Something Old, Something New* by Yvonne Lehman, and *Wrong Church, Wrong Wedding* by Loree Lough. These authors have practically become household names to romance readers, and this collection includes their photos and biographies. (352 pages, Paperbound, 5" x 8")

·······Heart♥ng·······

Any 12 Heartsong Presents titles for only $26.95 *

CONTEMPORARY ROMANCE IS CHEAPER BY THE DOZEN!

Buy any assortment of twelve Heartsong Presents titles and save 25% off of the already discounted price of $2.95 each!

**plus $1.00 shipping and handling per order and sales tax where applicable.

HEARTSONG PRESENTS *TITLES AVAILABLE NOW:*

(If ordering from this page, please remember to include it with the order form.)